"So what would you like to do tonight, Charlene?"

She didn't fail to note Drey had said her name with just the right amount of sugar-coating to spike her hormone level up a notch, and couldn't help wondering if it was deliberate. A man with as much skill and experience with women as he possessed had to know when he'd hit the jackpot.

She decided to call his bluff to see just how far he would take this and if he was trying to break down her defenses. "I don't know, Drey. What do you have in mind?" she asked in a voice so soft and seductive it didn't sound like her own.

She watched his eyes darken a little and saw the smooth smile that formed on his lips. "Something that might get the both of us in trouble. But I'm willing to take the chance."

Books by Brenda Jackson

Kimani Romance

Solid Soul
Night Heat
Risky Pleasures
In Bed with the Boss
Irresistible Forces
Just Deserts
The Object of His Protection

Kimani Arabesque

Tonight and Forever
A Valentine's Kiss
Whispered Promises
Eternally Yours
One Special Moment
Fire and Desire
Something to Celebrate
Secret Love
True Love
Surrender

Silhouette Desire

*Delaney's Desert Sheikh
*A Little Dare
*Thorn's Challenge
Scandal Between the Sheets
*Stone Cold Surrender
*Riding the Storm
*Jared's Counterfeit Fiancée
Strictly Confidential Attraction
Taking Care of Business
*The Chase Is On
*The Durango Affair
*Ian's Ultimate Gamble
*Seduction, Westmoreland Style
**Stranded with the
 Tempting Stranger
Spencer's Forbidden Passion
*Taming Clint Westmoreland
Cole's Red-Hot Pursuit

*Westmoreland family titles
**The Garrisons

BRENDA JACKSON

is a die "heart" romantic who married her childhood sweetheart and still proudly wears the "going steady" ring he gave her when she was fifteen. Because she's always believed in the power of love, Brenda's stories always have happy endings. In her real-life love story, Brenda and her husband of thirty-seven years live in Jacksonville, Florida, and have two sons.

A *New York Times* and *USA TODAY* bestselling author, Brenda divides her time between family and writing. She is retired from her thirty-seven year career in management at a major insurance company. You may write Brenda at P.O. Box 28267, Jacksonville, Florida 32226, e-mail her at WriterBJackson@aol.com or visit her Web site at www.brendajackson.net.

The Object of His Protection

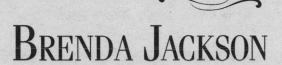

BRENDA JACKSON

KIMANI™
ROMANCE

To the love of my life, Gerald Jackson, Sr.

He catches the wise in their craftiness, and
the schemes of the wily are swept away.
Job 5:13 NIV

 KIMANI PRESS™

ISBN-13: 978-0-373-86088-3
ISBN-10:   0-373-86088-9

Special thanks and acknoledgment to Brenda Streater Jackson for her contribution to the Braddocks: Secret Son miniseries.

THE OBJECT OF HIS PROTECTION

Dear Reader,

I enjoy writing continuities since they give me the opportunity to work with other authors. I also like writing books in which there is a puzzle to solve, along with penning a love story that centers on family secrets, skyrocketing passion and endless love.

In my story, Drey is a man with secrets. He is also a man who has an ingrained desire to protect, and he finds himself protecting Charlene Anderson. Charlene is equally determined to prove to Drey that she does not need his protection. Drey has a puzzle to solve, which weaves itself into a murder mystery that I hope you enjoy.

I love writing romance stories in which the hero and heroine are pitted against each other, but in the end, the mystery is solved and true love prevails.

I hope you enjoy Drey and Charlene's story and their journey to finding everlasting love.

Brenda Jackson

Chapter 1

"I might as well come in since it doesn't appear that you're busy."

Charlene Anderson didn't need to look up to know who the deep, husky voice belonged to.

Drey St. John.

She did, however, glance over at the small heart-shaped ceramic clock sitting on her desk, the only part of her work area that wasn't buried under paperwork. Drey was early although his visit wasn't unexpected. He was a private investigator and she was a forensic scientist in Houston's coroner's office. It wasn't unusual for him to drop by occasionally to harass her for forensic information that would help with the investigation of his current case.

"If you think I'm not busy, St. John, look again," she said, not taking her eyes off the document she was reading. "Now get lost."

She knew he wouldn't go away. He never did. That didn't bother her since she had a weak spot for the rebel private investigator and actually looked forward to seeing him, although she would never admit such a thing to him. His visits were the only high point in her rather dull life. At twenty-seven, she was focused on work, and no matter how you looked at it, dead bodies didn't equate to great dates. Her social life was practically nonexistent, and of all things, she was still a virgin.

While attending Oklahoma State University, she had been too busy making the grades to get involved with anyone and had figured things would change once she finished school and got her career off the ground. She had been convinced, since she looked decent enough, that she would eventually meet some nice guy and get serious. That never happened. For her it always seemed to be all work and no play.

"Don't you ever get tired of messing around with the dead?"

She glanced up. Speaking of dead…Drey was drop-dead gorgeous. Definitely a living-breathing specimen of a sexy male. Tall, dark and ultrahandsome. There was no doubt about the fact that at thirty-three he was every woman's fantasy.

He had skin the color of creamy rich chocolate, and had dark hair and slanted dark eyes. All she knew about him was the tidbit she'd overhead from a group of women discussing him one day at lunch. According to them, his mother was half Chinese. If that was the case, she had passed a strikingly exotic look on to her son. Charlene had also heard that his middle name of Longwei meant "dragon strength" in Chinese. The name suited him because of his well-defined muscular physique.

"Not really," she finally said, taking her eyes off him and attempting to return her focus to the document in front of her. "At least I don't have to worry about the dead giving me a hard time."

"Yeah, I would imagine they wouldn't."

She didn't have to glance up to know he was no longer standing in the doorway but had come into her office. Her heart began beating twice as fast. The man had a way of getting to her. In addition to her erratic heartbeat, there was this unexplainable flush of heat that always overtook her whenever he was near, not to mention the way the air surrounding them always felt charged. He apparently didn't pick up on such vibes, nor did he notice she did. He was too busy trying to pump her for information.

When he halted before her desk, blocking her sunlight, she decided to glance up, but took a deep breath before doing so. "And what got you out of bed so early this morning?" she asked, and immediately she wished she hadn't when a vision of him getting out of bed—half naked—filtered through her mind. It was a nice vision but dangerous ground for her mind to tread on.

"I need your help with something."

She rolled her eyes. "What else is new?"

"You're the best there is," he said, smiling. She wished he wouldn't do that. He was sexy enough without the megawatt smile.

"Flattery will get you nowhere, Drey."

"What about dinner tonight?"

She placed her pen down and leaned back in her chair. "This must be some case if you're willing to spring for dinner."

She watched the emotions that crossed his face, emotions he rarely let show. He was angry and upset but was holding it in. Something about the case he was working on was bothering him. She could feel it.

"It is," he finally said. "And the answers may very well come from a stiff brought here last week by the name of Joe Dennis."

Charlene turned toward her computer and typed in the name. "Nothing has been done with him yet. He's on Nate's list to do later today." Nathaniel Ganders was her boss. "What exactly do you need to know?"

His tensed features relaxed somewhat when he said, "Anything you can tell me."

She nodded. He understood there were limitations as to what she could share, and she appreciated the fact that he had never asked her to cross the line in doing anything unethical. Not that she would. "In other words, anything out of the ordinary."

"Yes."

"Okay. I'll take a look at the report when Nate's finished. As you know, my boss is very thorough." She cleared her computer screen and turned back to him. "I'll let you know if I notice anything."

"Thanks, and I'm serious about dinner."

"But I'm not." It hadn't been the first time he had hinted at the two of them going somewhere to grab something to eat. She could barely handle her reaction to him now; she didn't want to think how things would be if she had to share a meal with him. Besides, she considered him business and she didn't mix business with pleasure. "Maybe some other time, Drey," she said, knowing it wouldn't happen.

"You said that before."

Not that she was foolish enough to think that it mattered to him. "And I'm saying it again. I'll call you if I learn anything."

"Thanks, Charlie. I would appreciate it."

Charlene glared at him, something she always did whenever he called her that. "Do I look like a Charlie to you?"

He smiled. "Hard to say. That lab jacket's all I've ever seen you wear."

Before she could give him a blazing retort, he turned and left.

The smile remained in place on Drey's lips as he got into his car. For some reason he enjoyed getting a rise out of Charlene. In fact, the thought of seeing her today had pretty much kept his anger at bay, although it was creeping back on him now. He was discovering that being lied to all his life was something he was having a hard time dealing with.

Before starting the engine, he sat still a moment and stared out of the windshield, thinking about the conversation he'd had with his mother, Daiyu Longwei, a few days ago. The conversation had practically shattered his world when she had told him that Ronald St. John was not his father. Instead, the man whom Drey had considered his mentor, Congressman Harmon Braddock, was actually his biological father.

His hands tightened on the steering wheel as his mother's words flowed through his mind.

Sighing deeply, Drey started the engine, thinking that in essence, he was investigating his own father's death. His own father's *murder,* he immediately corrected, since he was convinced Harmon Braddock's fatal car accident had been deliberate. Someone had wanted him dead and Drey was determined to find out who.

Something else he couldn't put out of his mind was that the very people who had hired him to find the truth were Harmon Braddock's offspring— and his siblings. He shook his head knowing they didn't have a clue as to what his relationship was to them. At some point he would have to tell them, but not now. He wasn't ready to go there yet. It was bad enough that he had to deal with it. Besides, how his own mother played into the investigation was still a mystery since it was well documented that less than an hour before his death, Harmon had tried contacting Daiyu. Hell, Drey hadn't known the two knew each other and none of the Braddocks knew that Daiyu was his mother. He didn't like withholding information of any kind from clients, yet that was exactly what he was doing.

He had known the congressman for a number of years. When Ronald St. John, the man Drey had adored as a father, had gotten killed in the line of duty as a police officer when Drey was fifteen, Drey had taken it hard since the two of them had always been close.

It was during that time that Congressman Braddock took an interest in him. And later on in life when Drey had felt himself getting tired of his own career as a police officer, it had been the congressman who had encouraged him to start his own private investigating firm and had gone so far as to keep him on retainer during those times he'd been trying to make ends meet. He would be the first to admit that over the years, Harmon had become the father figure that he'd lost.

To be quite honest, at first when he'd heard of Harmon's car accident he had no reason to suspect foul play, even when the other Braddocks had. But now Joe Dennis's death was raising his suspicions.

Drey brought the car to a stop at the next traffic light as he replayed the facts of the case over and over in his mind. Congressman Braddock had gotten killed in a car accident. The skid marks on the road had been consistent with a car losing control. It seemed Harmon was heading for the airport, which was another mystery since Gloria Kingsley, the congressman's executive assistant, who'd known Harmon's every move, hadn't known about any planned trip.

Another thing that baffled everyone was why the congressman was behind the wheel when his personal driver, Joe Dennis, usually drove Harmon everywhere he went.

And now Joe was dead and according to the police report there didn't appear to be any foul play. Someone just wanted him dead. Why? And exactly what had been the cause of death?

Drey had a lot of unanswered questions but at least he felt fairly confident the latter question would get answered soon enough, once he heard from Charlene. With that certainty, his thoughts couldn't help shift to the efficient forensic scientist. They might bicker every chance they got, but they understood each other. He was as dedicated to his profession as she was to hers.

In the two years he'd known her, he'd never met another no-nonsense woman quite like her, and he found her to be sharp, intelligent…and definitely beautiful. The latter he tried not to dwell on too much. Seeing her in that lab coat all the time should have been a turn off; instead it was a total turn-on because he often wondered just how she looked beneath it.

But what he liked most about her was that she didn't hesitate to give him hell if she thought he deserved it, and that made the verbal sparring with her that much more fun.

For some reason he had felt the need to see her this morning. Of course there had been that matter regarding Joe Dennis, but it seemed once his mother had hit him with the news of his parentage, he needed the lighthearted banter he and Charlene enjoyed to take his mind off things.

Lately, all of his relationships with women had been casual, just the way he wanted. He didn't have time for any type of serious indulgence, and the last thing he needed was a woman getting too clingy. He could tell that Charlene wasn't the clingy type. Besides that, their relationship was strictly professional. He had asked her out to dinner a few times, after the information she had given him had helped him solve a case, but she had refused and he hadn't had a reason to push.

Frowning, he turned the corner onto the road that would take him to his office. Later, he would drop by headquarters to check the police report again on Joe Dennis's death to see if he'd missed anything. Drey was determined to find out anything and everything that he could.

"I'm leaving to attend a meeting, Charlene. Don't stay too late."

She smiled as she glanced over at Nate Ganders as he slipped into his jacket. "I won't. In fact I intend to leave on time today."

When he tried smothering a cough, she said, "And please take my advice and do something for your cold. You're passing germs and I can't afford to get sick."

Nate's chuckle was the only sound he made before leaving the room. She stretched her legs, trying to recall just how long the two of them had worked together. Three years. He was an easy enough boss, although he could be demanding at times. The city had this thing about doing more with less, and amidst a number of budget cuts, the coroner's office was operating on slim funds that could barely keep up with the number of suicides

and suspicious deaths they handled each year.
Her only saving grace was that Nate left her alone
to do her job, and the nice salary increases she'd
gotten each year let her know her hard work and
dedication hadn't gone unnoticed.

Nate was a pleasant man, and a good father to
two children. And from the conversations Charlene had overheard, he was happily married to a
woman he'd adored for over twenty-five years.

Seeing it was almost five o'clock, she stood up
after logging off her computer. She then recalled
Drey's visit and what he had asked her to do.
Deciding now would be the best time since Nate
had left for a meeting, she went into the autopsy
room to take a look at Joe Dennis's chart. Nate
had just finished performing the autopsy on
Dennis, and the chart was still lying on the table.
She picked it up and began reading.

"Trauma to the head, consistent with an attack
from behind, as well as several other bruises to
neck and shoulders." She raised her brow at the
notation that a key had been removed from the
victim's stomach. She glanced over at the key
that was on the table. Why would anyone swallow
a key?

Deciding that was definitely something worth mentioning to Drey, she left the autopsy room, determined to call Drey once she got home. She was about to exit the room when she heard Nate talking loudly to another man. Odd, she thought, because in the three years she'd worked with Nate, she had never known him to raise his voice. And why had he returned in the first place? Most of the time his meetings lasted for an hour or longer.

She decided it was none of her business. Besides, she'd better leave before Nate found something else for her to do. As she headed for the door, she couldn't help noticing that the voices had gotten louder. She paused. Nate was definitely upset about something, but so was the man he was talking to. His voice was deep and sounded slightly hoarse. She could only assume, since she hadn't been sitting at her desk when Nate returned, that he thought she had left for the day. Not wanting to eavesdrop on Nate's argument any longer, she slipped out the door.

Drey heard his cell phone ring the moment he stepped out of the shower. Wrapping the towel around his waist, he quickly walked out of the bathroom to pick it up off the nightstand next to his bed. "Yes?"

"Drey, this is Charlene."

He felt his stomach churn and immediately thought, not for the first time, that she had such a sexy phone voice. There was just something about it that made goose bumps rise on his skin. Wanting to curb the boost to his testosterone level, he said, "Charlie."

She paused a moment, and he figured she'd done so to blow off a little steam, before saying, "I was able to take a look at Nate's report on Dennis."

The way she said the statement told him there was more. "And?"

"And I noticed a couple of things you might want to know."

"Such as?"

"There was trauma to the head consistent with some sort of an attack from behind."

Drey nodded. Not that the police had been much help, but he had paid a visit to headquarters after lunch hoping to learn something not on paper. For some reason it seemed everyone had closed lips. Usually they would loosen for a former member of their own, but today was not the case. And unfortunately, Detective Lavender Sessions, his former partner while on the force, was out of town. Like Charlene, Drey could always count on him to tell him what he needed to know.

"And there's something else pretty strange about Joe Dennis."

Charlene's statement cut deep into his thoughts. "What?"

"He swallowed a key."

"Excuse me?" Drey said, certain he hadn't heard her right.

"I said he swallowed a key. One was taken out of his stomach."

Drey rubbed his chin thoughtfully. "Are you sure?" Immediately, he knew he had made a mistake in asking her that. In all his dealings with Charlene he had come to realize that she was a professional who knew her business.

"Of course I'm sure. Not only did I read it in the report, but I saw it myself. Nate hadn't removed it from the table."

Drey didn't say anything for a moment; he was too busy thinking. Had Dennis swallowed the key to keep it from getting into someone else's hands? Was the key a link to Harmon's death? Those were questions he intended to get answered. "What sort of key was it?" he asked.

"Too small to be a door key. It was more like the size of a locker key or safe-deposit box key."

He rubbed his chin again, his curiosity igniting. "I need a copy of that key," he said, placing the phone on speaker so he could get dressed.

"That's not possible, Drey. I don't mind passing information on to you if I think it will help your case, but I draw the line at removing anything that could later become evidence."

"And I'm not asking you to," he said quickly.

"Well, what *are* you asking me to do?"

He could hear the agitation in her voice. The last thing he wanted to do was get her teed off, especially now when he needed information about that key. "I'm asking that you provide me a mold of it in wax. I've got a small kit that resembles a ladies' compact."

She didn't say anything for a moment, as if contemplating his request. And then she asked, "But what good is that when you don't know what the key goes to?"

"I'll find out. So will you get an indention of that key?"

"I don't know, Drey…."

"Please." If he sounded desperate, there was no help for it. He needed to know everything about Joe Dennis's death, especially now that he knew it hadn't been from natural causes.

He could hear her deep sigh and felt his heart begin to beat wildly in his chest. Even her sigh was a turn-on.

"Okay, fine," she said.

He couldn't help but smile. If he solved the case and was able to link it back to Harmon's death, then he owed her more than just dinner. "Meet me tonight so I can give the kit to you."

"Where?"

"You name the place. Better yet, if you give me your home address I can drop it off there."

He heard the hesitation in her voice and was about to throw out another option when she said, "That's fine, since I really don't want to go back out tonight. I live in the Rippling Shores Condos."

He knew the area. It was a newly developed subdivision of nice townhomes. "I know where it's located. What's the condo number?"

She rattled it off to him and he saved it in his memory. "I'll be there in less than an hour."

He smiled when, with not even a goodbye, she hung up the phone. For some reason he was looking forward to seeing her without her lab coat.

Chapter 2

Charlene glanced out the window and wondered for the umpteenth time why she had given Drey her address instead of meeting him somewhere. What had happened to her "do not mix business with pleasure" rule?

She was used to seeing him in a business setting, but now he would invade her personal space. The only consolation was that since he was dropping something off she wouldn't have to invite him inside.

Satisfied with that, she glanced down at herself. Okay, so she had decided to change out of the frayed pair of shorts and T-shirt she had put on after coming home into a skirt and blouse. No big deal. It wasn't as though he would see her in them. It was dark outside and all she had to do was poke her head out the door to get whatever he had to give her. Again, no big deal. She sighed deeply, thinking she was definitely making a lot out of things she considered to be no big deal.

When she heard a car door slam, her breath caught and for a moment she didn't move. She inhaled deeply, trying to control her racing pulse. There was no reason to get nervous and jittery. Drey St. John wasn't the first guy to come to her house…but she had to admit he was the first one in over a year, if you didn't count the serviceman who dropped by a few weeks ago to take a look at her computer when it had gone on the blink.

She didn't want to think about Carlos Hollis, the guy she had dated nearly two years ago. They had met at one of those financial seminars and she had taken him up on his offer to go somewhere for drinks afterward. They ended up going on a couple of dates after that, and when he began hinting that he wanted to sleep with her, she felt it was only fair to let him know up front that she was a virgin. He informed her that most guys were turned off by any virgin over the age of twenty-two, and to prove his point he never called her again.

Charlene heard the knock on the door and for a brief moment she contemplated not answering, which made absolutely no sense. *There is simply no reason for you to be nervous,* she told herself firmly as she headed toward the door. She reached for the doorknob and paused before turning it, convinced that even through the thickness of the wood that separated them she could breathe in Drey's scent. At least it was the scent that she always associated with him, robust and definitely manly. Drawing in a deep breath, she opened the door slightly and saw how the glow from the porch light lit his handsome features before she acknowledged him. "Drey."

"You shouldn't have opened the door until you were absolutely sure it was me, Charlie."

She thought about closing the door on him but decided she was a lot more mature than that. Instead, she opened it a little wider to place her arms across her chest and glare at him, or at least she tried to while attempting to downplay the heated sensations flowing through her. "The name is Charlene and I knew it was you."

"And how did you know that? I note you don't have a peephole in your door."

There was no way she would tell him that his scent had been a dead giveaway for her. "I just did. Now, if you don't mind, please give me what you drove all the way over here to deliver." She reached out her hand.

Instead of placing anything in her hand, he took her hand into his and looked at it. The moment he touched her she felt a slow sizzle move up her spine and she kept her body still, not to let him know the effect of his touch.

"You have pretty hands, Charlie."

She tensed at the compliment before pulling her hands from him. "Thanks, and how many times do I need to remind you that it's Charlene?"

Drey then glanced back at her and noted her stance and felt his temperature rise. There was just enough light from the lamppost to see her outfit. The skirt and blouse looked cute. No, they looked exquisite, in a subtle sort of way. His gaze moved down to her long, shapely legs.

His eyes met hers then as he decided he owed her an explanation for his intense scrutiny just now. "This is the first time I've seen you without a lab coat and you look different."

She lifted an arched brow. "Different how?"

"Different as in nice. Not that you didn't look nice before, mind you." *Nice* was too mild a word but he felt it would be out of place for him to say anything else. He doubted he could ever call her Charlie again without thinking how much like Charlene she now looked.

Whenever he dropped by the coroner's office she would be sitting behind her desk and wearing her lab coat with her hair twisted on top of her head in a ball. Now she was standing up and wearing a skirt and blouse with a mass of long light brown hair flowing around her shoulders. In his opinion the entire package was sexy.

Desire flowed hot and heavy through his veins and he downplayed his rapid breathing when he said, "So, what's a nice-looking girl like you doing home on a night like tonight? Why don't you have a date?"

Charlene's glare deepened. It was the same question her mother had asked her when she'd called earlier tonight. Nina Anderson-Smallwood-Caldwell-Olson actually thought a woman's life centered on a man. But after four marriages Charlene wasn't surprised her mother would think that. Her father was just as bad with wife number three. Since her parents seemed happy with their lives, she left them alone to do as they pleased and reminded them of their pledge on her twenty-first birthday to do likewise with her.

"I don't have a date because I don't want a date, so now give me the wax kit before I change my mind," she said, extending her hand back to him, hoping he didn't pull what he had before and take her hand again. His touch evoked feelings within her, unfamiliar feelings, feelings she could very well do without. When she was around him, a keen physical yearning seem to overtake her common sense, but she always fought to ignore it.

"Okay, here," he said, placing the item in her hand. She glanced down at it. He was right. It did resemble a small makeup compact.

"You want me to show you how to use it?"

She looked up at him. Was he looking for any excuse to come inside? She immediately dissed the thought. Why should he? Besides, she was certain she wasn't his type anyway. "No, I think I can handle it. It should be easy."

"It is. But even if it weren't I have a feeling you'd be able to handle it. In fact, Charlene Anderson, I think you can handle just about anything and anyone."

Another compliment—one laced with sexual innuendo? Or was she imagining things? Letting her mind jump to all kinds of conclusions? No, she decided after looking into his eyes, she wasn't imagining things. She might be a virgin but she wasn't naive. They had a routine of giving each other a hard time, but she was smart enough to recognize the sexual tension that existed between them.

Even now.

Was he throwing out a challenge? Could she handle him? She wanted to wrap her arms around herself to ward off the yearning she felt, but then she quickly decided that she had a right to experience these things. She was a woman, after all, and Drey was definitely a man who could make an impression on a woman. She didn't know any female who wouldn't be affected by the sheer maleness of him. He was dressed casually in a pair of jeans and a T-shirt. Both showed off an ultrafine body, one that probably spent a lot of time in a gym messing around with all kinds of machinery with the sole purpose of staying in shape. She could tell that whatever clothes he wore he was well-toned and filled them out with masculine perfection.

She suddenly felt the need to retreat, instinctively aware of a need to protect herself from him and from the things he was making her feel. But then another part of her wanted to explore those feelings, to discover—up to a point—all the things she hadn't experienced yet. Was she prepared for such a discovery?

"If you're certain I don't need to show you anything, I'll be going."

His words flowed through her mind, and her body picked up on the sensuality that laced his words. Again she wondered if she was imagining things. She studied his eyes. The slant in their shape made them look sexy and— Was that desire she saw in their dark depths? She shook her head, certain she was imagining things now. But then…

"Would you like to come inside for a drink, Drey?"

She inwardly flinched at the question, sure he had been asked that a thousand times by different women. He probably recognized it as the old "hit" line it was, one that had played out years ago, and was likely wondering if that was the best she could do. Unfortunately, it was. She didn't want to give the impression that she was anywhere close to being promiscuous or an easy mark, because she was far from it.

"I'd love to come in and share a drink with you, Charlene."

It hadn't gone unnoticed that he had called her Charlene this time instead of Charlie. His words, spoken in what she thought was an overly sexy tone, reeled in her thoughts and caused her to focus once again on his eyes. He was staring at her intensely, as if she was a puzzle he was determined to figure out. The thought bothered her until she felt surprised he was even taking the time to do so.

On their own accord her eyes then lowered to his mouth. When she thought of that mouth pressed against hers, a warm sensation flowed low in her belly.

Without saying anything, she took a step back inside the house and he followed.

* * *

Drey found himself drawn to Charlene's alluring sensuality as he stepped across the threshold into her home. With each step he took he felt something happening to him, something that could be perilous to his well-being as well as to his state of mind. Yet he was at a loss to stop it even with all the caution signs flashing at him.

He was used to women inviting him inside their homes with all kinds of intent and had always been careful to make sure it wasn't a setup of the worst kind. When it came to his sex life he maintained control. There was never a discussion on the matter. He chose his bed partners as meticulously and carefully as he chose anything else. He wasn't one to take anyone lightly. He could spot ulterior motives a mile away, and with the keen sense of a man who could most times read a woman like a book, he could figure out—even long before they could—if they wanted him.

Charlene wanted him but for what reason he wasn't sure. He wasn't even certain if she knew. There was something about her, something about her invitation to come in for a drink that made him smile. Most women he knew just came right out and asked at the end of the date, "Would you like to come in for sex?" They didn't beat around the bush about anything and usually by the time the door closed behind him they had stripped naked.

He glanced across the room at Charlene. She was fully clothed and the thought flitted through his mind that he would give anything to see her naked. Seeing her without her lab coat was an eye-opener. Removing her clothes was a boner just waiting to happen. Even now he could feel desire flowing through him. Heated lust that was increasing the flow to his brain up north and a certain other body part down south. Whether Charlene knew it or not, she was an extremely desirable woman. Why had she kept it hidden?

"So, what would you like?"

Her words pulled in his thoughts and immediately a vision flashed across his mind. Sexual imagery, hot and enticing, shot through his brain and threatened to short-circuit his nerve endings.

"What would I like?" he asked, shooting the question back at her, pausing to fully enunciate, sensually articulate every single word. He watched her tense as she realized she had unintentionally set herself up for that one.

She tilted her head at an angle he thought was sexy and glared at him. "What would you like to drink?"

He smiled, tempted to tell her sipping on her would satisfy him rather nicely, but decided not to do so. He might be wrong, way off base, but he had a feeling she was trying to downplay a certain innocence about her, while at the same time trying to prove something. What? And to whom?

"I'll take anything you have," he finally got around to answering. "But I prefer a beer if you have one."

She nodded. "Yes, I have one. I'll be back in a second."

He heard panic in her voice and when she left the room he shook his head. Did she think he would pounce on her the first chance he got? She had been the one to invite him in.

He smiled thinking he might not pounce on her right away, but he intended to kiss her before he left. For a long time he had wondered how her lips tasted and he intended to find out tonight. Her lips had always intrigued him, had always turned him on even when they had been discussing dead bodies.

Dead bodies.

He remembered one in particular. Joe Dennis. His concentration should be focused on working his investigation and not working Charlene. He sucked in air, trying to get a grip. Instead he got a whiff of Charlene's scent. It was all over the place. Jasmine.

He moved to the center of the room and looked around. She had a cozy place, nicely decorated, not overly furnished and crowded. It looked lived-in in a feminine way with splashes of pastel colors blended with the boldness of some darker shades. He noted that her preference in style leaned toward Early American while his remained staunchly Asian. He thought it was an interesting contrast.

"Sorry I took so long."

He turned to face Charlene and swallowed hard, while fighting back the sensations that suddenly engulfed him. Compared to him she seemed to be a tiny thing, no taller than five three if that. His six-four height seemed to all but tower over her. And then there was the way she filled out her skirt and blouse. She was just as shapely up top as she was around the hips. Usually, he didn't make a habit out of sizing up a woman's breasts, but with the way hers filled her blouse he couldn't help doing so. He had seen her many times, but because of the way she normally wore her hair, he hadn't noticed the red highlights in her hair and what they did to her medium brown complexion.

"No problem," he answered as he took the beer bottle from her, deciding he needed to remember the reason he was there and take care of it and leave. There was no need wasting time thinking about how good she looked or just how delicious he figured she would taste. He had an important case to solve and didn't have time for anything else, especially anything involving a woman.

"You have a nice place," he said before popping the cap off the beer bottle and taking a long, needed gulp. It immediately quenched his thirst but did nothing to wipe away his desire. He had focused on her mouth too many times not to know a sampling of her taste was what he really needed.

"Thanks. It's just right for me. Not too big and not too small."

It was then that Drey noticed she hadn't grabbed a beer for herself. "You aren't drinking anything?"

She shook her head. "No, I don't drink much."

He licked his lips, aware more than ever of her femininity. And just to think seeing her without a lab coat and wearing regular clothes could have this sort of effect. "So, what else don't you do, Charlie?" There, he figured calling her by the name she disliked would get her dander up and put back up the space he wanted between them. Thinking of tasting her all over wasn't a good thing.

Charlene glared at him and said, "I definitely don't do guys who can't seem to get my name right."

Too late Charlene was aware of how that sounded, which was pretty bad considering she'd never done a guy at all. But Drey didn't know that. The way his brows rose indicated he was evidently intrigued by her statement.

"So," he said, dragging out the single word and looking at her with those deep, dark, slanted eyes that made heat stir in the pit of her stomach. "Do you *do* guys who get your name right?"

Charlene's glare deepened. The last thing she would admit to him was that she didn't do guys at all. Carlos's abrupt departure proved what guys thought of overaged virgins. "That's none of your business."

He placed the beer bottle on the table beside him before taking a step closer to her. The heat she felt earlier intensified into a hot flame. "And what if I were to tell you, Charlene, that I intend to make it my business?"

Charlene swallowed. He had taken that step with such confidence and style that if she didn't know herself as well as she did, she would be tempted to believe him, especially with the way he said her name whenever he did get it right. She hadn't realized just how close he was standing until she tilted her head and met his gaze, trying to ignore the strong, masculine shoulders the top of her head barely hit. "If you were to tell me that, Drey, then I would warn you that you would do better sticking to solving your cases since you have a better chance there," she said, not wavering when she looked into his eyes.

A smile touched his lips and she knew he didn't intend to heed her warning. "Are you saying that I don't have a chance with you?" he asked.

She rolled her eyes. She'd had enough of his

game playing. "Do you honestly think I'm gullible enough to believe that you even want one?"

She gasped when suddenly she was pulled into his strong arms and her body was pressed against his hard, solid frame. She thought she would melt right then and there when his eyes bored down at her. Why did he always manage to get such a strong reaction from her?

"There's nothing gullible about it, Charlene," he said, leaning down just inches from her lips. "It's what most people call sexual attraction. We got it. We've had it from the first. Now the big question is, what are we going to do about it?"

"Nothing." She whispered the word from lips that suddenly felt dry.

"I disagree," he said, smiling confidently with a challenging glint in his eyes.

And then his mouth swooped down on hers, snatching her next breath and replacing it with a demanding, hot mouth. She heard herself moan and tried not to return his kiss but found herself doing so anyway. The moment his tongue touched hers, she could swear her panties got wet. And she was certain that the room was moving. His kiss, intense and deep, was leading her down a road she didn't know. All she knew was that he was taking her mouth with an expertise that had her following, no matter where he led.

Of their own accord she felt her arms wrap around his neck. Lifting her arms caused the tips of her breasts to press deep into his chest. It was as if the material of his T-shirt served as no barrier at all and for all her breasts cared, she was touching bare skin. The touch inflamed her nipples and sent a heated, electrifying charge all the way to the juncture of her thighs. She didn't want to think about that. In fact, she didn't want to think at all. She didn't. She let his mouth have its way, while hers did the same.

Drey deepened the kiss thinking it had been long in coming and was bound to happen sooner or later. He was grateful it was now. He had so much drama going on in his life, disappointments and confusion about a lot of things concerning his birth. But he wasn't confused about this, the way his mouth had latched on to Charlene's, or the enjoyment he was getting from tasting her this way. In his book, she tasted pretty damn good. Too good. Her mouth was a temptation he'd better walk away from here and now. But he didn't want to stop just yet.

The backfiring of a car in the distance took the choice out of his hands. With the sound came the return of his senses, but not before he let his tongue swipe across her lips for one final taste. He smiled. She looked as if she was shocked, not by the kiss but at its intensity. What he felt was resentment—toward whoever owned the damn vehicle that had interrupted them.

"I think you should go now, Drey."

He sighed, not wanting to go but knowing she was right. If he stayed, the next move was to get them both naked. "All right."

To get some sort of normalcy back between them, where he could take his mind off their kiss, he said, "Are you sure you know how to use the kit?"

She nodded. "Yes, I'm sure."

He lifted a brow, surprised she hadn't given him some smart comeback. "Okay, then. I'll check with you tomorrow."

He turned and walked toward the door thinking this was the most excitement his libido had endured in a long time. Over the past year he had been too busy for a social life and Charlene just proved there were advantages to mixing business with pleasure at times.

He stopped when he got to the door and glanced back over at her. She was standing in the same spot staring at him. Just so she would know, he told her what he was thinking. What he had suddenly made up his mind about. "That wasn't the last kiss we'll share, Charlene."

He saw her eyes narrow. "Yes, it was."

He gave her an easy smile. "No, it wasn't. In fact I won't be totally satisfied until I've gotten the chance to taste you all over."

And then he opened the door and left.

Chapter 3

Charlene held the phone tight in her hand as she let the caller on the other end have her say. This was certainly not turning out to be a good day. She had awakened that morning in a bad mood after a sleepless night, not having been able even to close her eyes without memories of Drey's kiss intruding. What on earth had enticed her to go that far with him? And then his final comment before leaving…"I won't be totally satisfied until I've gotten the chance to taste you all over."

Sensual shivers shot up her spine whenever she thought about it.

The irritated voice pulled her back to the conversation. Marsha Crenshaw was an attorney from the district attorney's office inquiring about a body whose autopsy should have been completed that morning. It was on Nate's list to do, but for some reason he was running behind schedule. In fact, Charlene had only seen him once that day and he'd seemed somewhat agitated about something.

"I'm sure the report will be finished by the end of the day, Marsha. If not, I'll have Nate give you a call." Charlene quickly hung up thinking the woman was getting pushier every time they talked. Rumor had it that she had lost so many cases that the particular one she was now working on was considered a must-win for her.

With Marsha off the phone and everyone out to lunch, Charlene leaned back in her chair to grab a quiet moment. Once again her thoughts drifted to what had happened last night between her and Drey. She would be the first to admit that the kiss had come as a surprise. She certainly hadn't expected it, nor had she done anything to provoke it. What she had done was give him a smart comeback after he'd said that he intended to make it his business to know whether or not she did guys who got her name right. Things had gotten crazy from there and eventually led to a kiss she couldn't forget.

Something else she couldn't forget was agreeing to make an indention of that key. She had gotten busy earlier and it had slipped her mind. Thinking this would be a good time to do it since Nate was at lunch, she opened the drawer to her desk where she kept her purse. A few minutes later with the wax kit Drey had given her last night she entered the autopsy room where the records were located. She opened the huge file drawer and pulled out a folder with Joe Dennis's name on it and was surprised the key was not in a plastic bag inside the folder. Wondering why, she began reading Dennis's chart.

"What in the world…"

She blinked, certain she wasn't reading the chart correctly. Nate's report, the one that had been released to the police earlier that day, indicated Joe Dennis had died of a heart attack. The report contained no mention of the trauma to the head or the key that was found in his stomach.

And speaking of the key, where was it? she asked herself as she quickly flipped through the chart. And why would Nate release a report that didn't come close to the truth?

"Is there anything in particular you're looking for, Charlene?"

Charlene almost jumped at the sound of Nate's voice, then breathed in deeply. She hadn't expected him to return from lunch so soon. She glanced over at him and noticed he was looking at her rather funny. His smile, she noted, didn't quite reach his eyes. He had caught her snooping in the file drawer containing the cases he had worked and he was probably wondering whose file she had. She saw no reason not to tell him since she was curious as to why he had falsified the information on Dennis's autopsy report.

She cleared her throat. "I was reading your final report on Joe Dennis," she said, placing the report back in the cabinet drawer and then closing and relocking it. She glanced up and saw a frown settle on his features.

"Why would you concern yourself with Joe Dennis's autopsy?"

She heard the tenseness in his voice. She also

heard a hardness that had never been there before, except for that one time she had overheard him arguing with some man.

"Just curious," she said, refusing to let him know about Drey's request. He'd seen Drey around but had probably assumed he was dropping by to see her for personal reasons.

"And you were curious because…" he prompted.

She met his gaze. "Because I saw the body, Nate, and I know Joe Dennis didn't die of a heart attack. There was trauma to—"

"There was no trauma," he all but snapped. "Are you questioning my findings?"

Yes, I am, Charlene thought. She *was* questioning his findings because he knew as well as she did that they were wrong. "All I know, Nate, is what I saw. Someone had hit Dennis over the head."

"You are mistaken, Charlene, and that's the end of it," he said with a finality in his tone, while coming close to raising his voice. "And I would appreciate it if you never go checking behind me again."

"I wasn't doing that, Nate."

"Weren't you?"

Charlene really didn't know what to say. All

she knew, all she was definitely sure about was that the report Nate had issued to the police was wrong. Why would he do such a thing? Why was he trying to convince her it was right when she knew what she saw? And what about the key that had been taken out of the man's stomach? There was no mention of it. She had a funny feeling about this and the intense way Nate was looking at her wasn't helping. Still, she wasn't dissuaded by his words. She knew what she saw and she intended to get to the bottom of it.

"Great," she muttered as she headed out of the room. "I guess I was mistaken." But she didn't mean it. She needed to talk to Drey right away.

"Charlene."

She stopped and turned to Nate before reaching the door. "Yes?"

"I think you should take some time off. In fact I strongly suggest that you do. You need time to clear your head since you're imagining things."

Charlene held back from telling him all the things that concerned her. She tilted her head and studied him and suddenly felt uneasy. There was a reason he wanted her gone for a while and they both knew it had nothing to do with her imagination.

"And it will be time off with pay," he said, as if that meant something.

It was an effort not to tell him just what he could do with the time off with pay, but she bit her tongue to stop from doing so. Instead she walked out of the room.

A few minutes later after removing the items from her desk that she wanted to take with her she paused before entering Nate's office when she saw he was on the phone. She couldn't help but notice how quickly he ended the call when he saw her.

"Yes, Charlene?"

"I transferred my reports to Miller to work while I'm gone just in case someone needs a follow-up."

"Okay."

She inhaled deeply, then said, "What's going on, Nate? Why are you—"

"I don't want anything about Joe Dennis to go any further. You're wrong in what you thought you saw," he said, cutting in.

Forcing a smile, she said, "Fine. I'll see you in two weeks."

"Make it three and you might want to take the opportunity to go visit your parents while you have the time."

Charlene frowned. Why was he suggesting that she leave town? "That sounds like a good idea, Nate. I'll see you when I get back."

As soon as possible, she needed to talk to Drey.

Drey studied the man who was standing at the window staring out as if he was in deep thought. Drey recalled just what he knew about Malcolm Braddock, other than his most recent discovery that the man was his half brother…something Malcolm didn't know.

Malcolm assumed like his other two siblings— Tyson and Shondra—that Drey had been nothing more to their father than a mentee, someone Harmon Braddock had taken an interest in. They had no idea that their father had had an affair with his mother thirty-three years ago. It was the year before Malcolm had been born.

Although it had never bothered him before, now Drey felt a sense of loss that while he had gotten to know Harmon over the years, he hadn't been given the chance to form any sort of relationship with his siblings. He inhaled deeply thinking there was still a lot of information his mother hadn't told him. After she had dropped the bomb on him a few days ago regarding his true relationship with Harmon, he had left her office both confused and angry. He had deliberately avoided talking to her since that day, but he knew he could no longer avoid her. His questions needed answering. He had a case to solve and it was an investigation that had gone from business to personal. He was anxious to get that call from Charlene about that key.

Charlene.

His thoughts automatically shifted away from Malcolm to her, especially the kiss they had shared last night. He felt a tightening in his groin just thinking about it. Hell, he had barely gotten any sleep last night for thinking about it, replaying every aspect of it in his mind and finally drifting off to sleep with the taste of her still very much a part of his palate. It still *was*. The donut and coffee he'd consumed for breakfast hadn't erased it.

And then there was the way she had felt in his arms, the way her body had automatically adjusted against his, raising his desire to a level it hadn't been at in a while. Because of his workload, he hadn't had time to spend with a woman, and last night Charlene had reminded him just how long it had been. A year, he had determined, was too long to go without female companionship, namely a good, hard roll in the hay.

He decided to get his mind off Charlene and back on Malcolm. He was still silently standing at his office window, evidently trying to make sense of this entire investigation and probably asking himself who would want his father dead.

Drey leaned back in his chair thinking that from the time he'd come to know Malcolm he'd always thought of him as a likeable guy. Drey was also aware of the rift that had existed between Malcolm and Harmon for years, namely because Malcolm thought that Harmon had "sold out" to play the political game. That was something Malcolm could not tolerate because of his ingrained sense of right and wrong. The man was extremely smart and in a lot of ways he reminded Drey of Harmon in that Malcolm was headstrong, he liked to debate and was passionate about his beliefs.

Something else that Malcolm seemed passion-ate about was the woman he was engaged to marry,

Gloria Kingsley. Gloria had been Harmon's executive assistant. Drey knew that Gloria had been instrumental in getting Malcolm to assume a leadership role in the Braddock family as well as to run for his father's now-vacant seat in Congress.

The special election was to be held at the end of the month, and recent polls showed Malcolm was ahead of his opponent, Clint Hardy, who was running a negative campaign. With the election so close at hand, as well as the investigation into his father's death, Malcolm pretty much had his hands full. No wonder he was standing at the window staring out, and had been that way since Drey had arrived almost ten minutes ago.

However, no matter the outcome of the election or the investigation, the one thing Drey knew for certain was that Malcolm would be marrying Gloria next month on Christmas Day.

As if on cue, Malcolm turned his head and looked at him, meeting his gaze. Drey wondered if there was anything—his facial bone structure, his strong chin or full cheekbones that would give his secret away and make it obvious to Malcolm that they shared the same blood. Drey knew there was not. Other than his skin coloring and full lips, most of his features were Asian.

"So, you think this key that was taken out of Dennis is connected to Dad's death?" Malcolm asked, coming to sit back down at his desk.

"I would have to say yes since not too many people make a habit of going around swallowing keys."

Malcolm nodded, then leaned back in his chair and made a steeple with his fingers. "I was standing over there trying to recall just when Dennis started working for Dad and if in the past I've ever had a reason to question his loyalty. But then it's not like Dad and I were close over the last few years for me to get to know any of his associates or employees." A smile touched his lips when he added, "Other than Gloria. She used to be quite a sticky thorn in my side."

Drey raised a brow. "How so?"

"As his executive assistant, she thought my old man walked on water, refused to see his faults like I did. And she resented me for walking away from my father and my family."

"Why did you?"

If Malcolm thought the question odd coming from a person who had no connection to the family, who was merely someone that he and his siblings had hired to investigate their father's death, he gave no indication of it. Instead he said, "Despite my privileged upbringing, I've always been drawn to those in need and always wanted to help those less fortunate. A few years ago a bill came across my father's desk that would have helped a lot of needy families—a bill that my dad himself had once championed. I couldn't take any more of him not practicing what he preached."

"So you walked away from the family."

"Yes. Although I kept in touch with my mother and siblings, I couldn't find it in my heart to forgive Dad for what he did by turning his back on so many who needed him to make a difference. I loved him, but I just couldn't accept the political behavior my father was practicing. In my eyes he was becoming involved in the dirty side of politics and I couldn't turn my head and pretend he wasn't."

"What about Tyson and Shondra? Did they break their relationship with your father as well?" Drey asked, thinking that the Harmon Braddock whom Malcolm had just described was not the one he had known.

"Not as clean as I did. And unable to deal with

the tension between me and Dad, they threw themselves into their careers."

Drey nodded. "So you and the congressman were not on good terms when he died?"

Malcolm held his gaze. "No, and if your next question is going to ask me if I had anything to do with the accident—"

"No, I wasn't going to ask you that, Malcolm. That hadn't crossed my mind. I was at the funeral, remember? I saw how badly you took the congressman's death. The two of you may have had your differences, but you loved your father."

Malcolm didn't say anything for a moment, and then, "Yes, I did."

Before Drey could say anything else, his cell phone rang and he stood to retrieve it from his pocket and flipped it open. "Excuse me," he said to Malcolm before glancing down at his phone. He was surprised to see his caller was Charlene. He hadn't expected to hear from her until later that day. "This is Drey. What do you have for me?"

"Trouble. Can we meet somewhere and talk?"

Chapter 4

Drey walked into the coffee shop and glanced around, then sighed with relief when he saw Charlene. She had refused to go into any details over the phone, but he had heard the nervousness in her voice.

As he headed toward her table in the back of the restaurant, he knew she hadn't seen him yet, which gave him the chance to study her. Looking every bit of eighteen instead of twenty-seven, she wore dark brown slacks and a beige cotton blouse.

He was still finding it odd seeing her without her lab coat, although he was enjoying doing so.

His face went back to hers and he saw she was wearing very little makeup. She didn't need any either. Something nagged inside him, reminding him of their kiss and causing sensations to flow through him. He frowned. Now was not the time to remember how she had felt in his arms or how she had tasted in his mouth. He was in the throes of an investigation that seemed to be getting more complicated by the second and the last thing he needed was thoughts of getting Charlene Anderson in his bed.

He wasn't surprised that he wanted to take her to bed. After all, he was a hot-blooded male who enjoyed sex as much as the next guy. Unlike most guys, though, he wasn't getting any on a regular basis and seeing Charlene was reminding him of that fact.

As if she sensed his presence, she tilted her head in his direction and their gazes met. While lust was probably glinting in his eyes, he saw something altogether different in hers. There was anxiousness there, a tenseness that immediately pushed any thoughts of sex from his mind...for the time being. Instead he couldn't help but wonder what had her so worried.

"Charlie?" he said, sliding into the seat beside her. And he knew whatever was bothering her was massive because for the first time she didn't glare at him for the use of his play name for her. "What's wrong? What kind of trouble were you alluding to earlier?"

She took a sip of her coffee before putting her cup down and giving him her complete attention, turning those intense, beautiful eyes on him. "Nate caught me going through Dennis's file." She paused a second before asking, "Are you aware what Nate stated in the report he released to the police earlier today?"

When he couldn't stop drowning in the allure of her eyes quickly enough to respond, she said, "It said Joe Dennis's death was the result of a heart attack."

That got his absolute attention. "What!"

"You heard me," she said tersely.

He frowned. "Why would he lie about such a thing?"

She shook her head. "I have no idea. I saw Joe Dennis's body, Drey. I saw the bruises and I saw the key. Now the key is nowhere to be found."

Drey didn't say anything but it was clear from what Charlene was saying that a cover-up of some sort was going on. Why had Charlene's boss lied about the cause of Joe Dennis's death?

Drey looked at Charlene. He saw the nervous way she lifted her cup to her lips to take a sip of her coffee. There was more. He felt it. "What did he say when you questioned him about it?" he asked. There was no need to ask if she had questioned him because he knew that she had. It would go against her grain not to do so.

She met his gaze again. "He denied it. He said I'd made a mistake about what I thought was the reason Dennis died. Then he suggested that I take time off to clear my head. Three weeks. And he went on to suggest that I leave town."

She paused for a moment and then added, "Something is going on, Drey, something that I don't like. Nate was acting strange. Creepy. It's like he was warning me off, making veiled threats, alluding that disappearing for a while would be in my best interest. I think we should go to the police."

"No," he said, squashing that idea quickly. "You're right, something is going on, but I don't think going to the police is the answer, especially when they are the ones backing up a faulty report. It can't help but make you wonder if perhaps they are somehow involved."

He saw the way Charlene was looking at him and knew he had gotten her to thinking the way he was doing now. Until they uncovered more information they were on their own. Then another thought entered his mind regarding the veiled threats her boss had made. If there had been foul play in Joe Dennis's death, more than likely that meant Congressman Braddock's death was no accident either. And if someone was out for more blood as a way to keep things quiet, Charlene could very well get caught in the crossfire and he refused to let that happen.

"Are you planning to take your boss up on his offer and leave town?" he asked, taking a sip of the ice-cold water a waitress had placed in front of him.

"No."

He hadn't thought so. "Disappearing for a while might not be such a bad idea, Charlene."

He watched as a frown formed around her lips. They were lips he had tasted last night and would love sampling again today. "What good will disappearing do?" she asked.

He had a quick answer for her. "It might keep you alive. Think about it. Without evidence we don't have proof of anything and who's going to take your word over your boss's? And if there is a cover-up, then whoever is behind it got to your boss somehow, and there's a possibility the police are somehow connected."

She shook her head. "What you're saying doesn't make sense. Why would anyone be interested in what happened to Joe Dennis and why go to that extreme with me, Drey? If there's more to this mystery I would appreciate hearing it."

He knew that was fair enough since, thanks to him, she might have unknowingly placed her life in danger. After the waitress came to take his drink order, he said, "Joe Dennis was the personal driver of Congressman Harmon Braddock. As you know, the congressman was killed in an auto accident a few months ago. I was hoping that Dennis could shed some light as to why the congressman was driving his own car that night instead of Dennis and—"

"Wait! Hold up. Back up," Charlene said, using her hand to give him a time-out signal. "Are you saying what I think you're saying?"

"Yes. I have reason to believe the congressman's death was intentional."

Charlene didn't know what to say. Like everyone else in Houston, she had read about the congressman's car accident but hadn't had a reason to think much about it. "And is that what you're investigating?"

"Yes. I was hired by his family. When they approached me I was doubtful that I would find anything, but after Joe Dennis died mysteriously I really got suspicious. And now…"

She nodded and waited until the waitress had placed his beer in front of him before saying, "But it's hard for me to believe that Nate could be involved. He's a family man with a wife and children."

"Yes, but what if the person behind all this is using blackmail or threats? Nate warned you to disappear and you would be wise to heed his warning."

Charlene nibbled on her bottom lip. A part of her knew Drey was probably right, but another part didn't want to disappear. She wanted to go to work, continue her life as she knew it. Besides, where would she go? She could go visit her mother and her new husband in Florida, but she preferred not to. And her father's place in Detroit with his wife of three years was a definite no-no since she and Monica could only tolerate each other in small doses.

"Okay, I'm convinced you might be right about me getting lost for a while," she finally said. "Especially now that I remember the argument Nate was having with that man."

Drey frowned as he glanced over at her. "What argument?"

She took another sip of her coffee before answering. "A few days ago. In fact it was the same day I discovered the key. Nate thought I had already left for the day, but I was in the autopsy room snooping around. When I came out I heard Nate and another man arguing. They were practically yelling at each other."

"Do you know what about?"

"No. I didn't stick around long enough to find out. However, at the time I thought it rather strange for Nate to be arguing with anyone since he has a tendency not to get upset about anything. He's always said it's not good to get stressed."

"Did he act upset with you today when he discovered you going through Dennis's chart?"

Charlene sighed deeply as she remembered her and Nate's conversation. "Not as much upset as he was nervous, like he hated me finding out the truth. He was trying so hard to convince me that I was wrong. It was rather creepy seeing him that way."

Drey didn't say anything as he studied her. Yes, her disappearing for a while was for the best considering everything she had told him. If someone was out for more blood, he didn't want it to be Charlene's. The thought of anything happening to her didn't sit too well with him and he wasn't about to take any chances.

He leaned back in his chair. "How long will it take you to pack?"

She lifted her head from studying the contents of her coffee cup and met his gaze. "Am I supposed to be going somewhere?"

"Yes."

She arched a brow. "Where?"

"My place. For your safety, I think it's best for you to move in with me for a while."

Chapter 5

Charlene blinked. "Excuse me?"

Drey knew she had heard him but figured what he'd said deserved repeating so there wouldn't be any misunderstandings. "I said I think it would be for the best if you were to move in with me for a while."

She frowned, actually glared at him. "Thanks, but no, thanks. I have my own place."

He leaned back in his chair and before taking another swig of beer he said, "It's not safe to disappear there, Charlie."

She gave him a disapproving glare. "The name is Charlene and I see no reason I can't stay put."

"I can name several reasons and none of them is pretty. In fact all of them are rather dangerous, to say the least. If Nate has mentioned to anyone that you know anything, they'll figure it's best for you to become a casualty."

The thought of that happening made her skin crawl. "But why would he do that?"

"For the same reason he gave you a clear warning, which he really didn't have to do. Whatever he's into, he's in it over his head and trying not to get you involved. Think about it, Charlie. We're not talking about the cover-up of just anyone's murder. We're talking about the cover-up of the murder of a well-known politician, a congressman." *My biological father,* he didn't add as he looked down at his drink.

His true relationship to Harmon Braddock was still rather new to him and he still had a number of questions he wanted answered. The only person who could do that was his mother. He had tried calling her that morning and hadn't been able to get a hold of her. He knew she was deliberately avoiding him, trying to evade his questions.

"Did you know him?"

Drey glanced back at Charlene when her question invaded his thoughts. "Who?"

"Congressman Braddock."

Drey didn't say anything at first, tempted to tell her just how well he knew him, but instead said, "Yes, for years he had been my mentor."

"Why?"

He lifted a brow. "Why what?"

"How did you get a U.S. congressman to be your mentor?"

Drey sighed. That was a good question, one he hadn't thought of before. He couldn't help wondering if anyone else was curious about that same thing. The Braddock siblings perhaps? They had known of his relationship to their father, but none of them had ever asked why and how it had come about.

A part of him would never forget that day right after his father had died and he'd been walking home from school when suddenly a big black shiny car had pulled up beside him and come to a stop. Suddenly the back passenger door opened and a man stepped out. It was a man whom he had never seen before, but the man knew him because he had called him by name. That was the day Harmon Braddock had become a part of his life. Drey could truly say that although Harmon had never claimed him publicly as his son, he had done enough for him behind the scenes to engrave his presence and existence into Drey's life. And no matter what, he owed it to the man who was his biological father to bring to justice anyone responsible for his death. Just as he felt he owed it to Charlene to keep her safe.

"Drey?"

Drey realized he hadn't answered Charlene's question. "He had been a family friend," he said simply, hoping she didn't want any more details than that.

"It must be hard on you to investigate his death, knowing how close the two of you were."

"Yes, it's hard. Just like it's hard for me to turn my back on the fact that your life might now be in danger because of me."

"It's not."

"You don't know that for certain. Whoever is responsible for the congressman's death didn't hesitate to kill Joe Dennis, probably because they thought he knew too much. Evidently he did to have put a key in his stomach. I wish there is a way we can get our hands on it. Are you sure your boss had taken it out of Dennis's file already?"

"I didn't see it. He might have passed it on to an interested party or it might be in Nate's office somewhere. He has a habit of getting busy and leaving stuff around at times. That's how I came across the key in the first place."

Drey nodded, very much aware she had not yet agreed to move in with him until his investigation has been resolved. Of course she could very well move in with family or friends, but for some reason he felt he might need her around if he had additional questions about what she'd seen in her boss's original report.

"I can't force you to move in with me, Charlene," he decided to say to bring the matter up once again.

She gave a little laugh, one that he found rather sexy. So sexy he could feel the tightening of his abdominal muscles. "I'm glad you know that, Drey."

His mouth quirked. So she wanted to play hard. He would show her just how hard he could make things. "But I can move in with you." He watched the frown that formed around her lips.

Lips he could distinctly remember tasting last night. Lips that he could honestly say he would love sampling again.

"No, you can't."

"Yes, I can, and haven't we been down this road before? I can appoint myself as your bodyguard. If you don't let me stay inside your place, I can always sleep outside in the car just as long as I keep an eye on you. And I hope you'll think twice before calling the police since right now we don't know whose side they're on."

She tilted her chin and he thought it was another sexy move. "You are so quick to think the worst of them, yet you used to be one of them," she said.

He couldn't help but wonder how she knew he used to be a part of the force, but decided he would find out later after they moved in together. "Because I used to be one of them I know there are good cops and there are bad cops. My father was a good cop. My partner and I were good cops and there are others I can vouch for. But I can't and won't vouch for every one of them, and I don't plan on taking a chance by letting you assume you won't become a target. So I'm going to ask you again. Do you move in with me or do I move in with you?"

"I won't even consider such a thing until we get something straight."

"Like what?"

"Like the threat you made last night."

He had an idea what she was talking about, but he didn't consider those words a threat. He considered them a fact. "And what threat was that?" he asked, feeling an intense thudding of his pulse.

She hesitated, then expounded in a low voice. "The one you made after we kissed. What you planned to do the next time."

"As far as I know there's no law against saying something you intend to make happen eventually. But if it makes you feel better, I promise not to touch you until you're good and ready. It will be your call."

"Then I don't have anything to worry about," she said triumphantly, as if all was well.

"And why do you say that?"

She tilted her head and said in an irritated tone, "Because I've never been that forward with a man."

He shrugged, not the least bothered by her attitude. "You will with me. I'll encourage it."

Charlene snorted. "Encourage what you want, it still won't happen."

He decided to set her straight about a few things so they could move on. "Since the first there has been sexual chemistry between us and we both know it. The reason we bicker back and forth as much as we do is to play it off. All I'm saying, Charlene, is that us being sexually attracted to each other is a fact, just like the fact that your life may be in danger. My main concentration now is to make sure nothing happens to you and to complete my investigation. You have no reason to fear me because I want you. I won't touch you unless you say it's okay and if you're certain you won't be doing that, then there shouldn't be a problem."

He saw the expression on her face and knew she was about to put up yet another fight. She was one stubborn female and at any other time he would have appreciated that quality since he didn't run across many women like her. Most of them, he found, gave in too easily, especially when it came to him.

When time ticked by and she still didn't say anything, he said, "Okay, just don't be surprised when you find me parked outside your house tonight. As of this very minute I become your bodyguard."

Her gaze narrowed. "You can't watch me every minute while investigating the case," she said smartly.

He smiled. "Yes, you're right. I guess I'll just have to drag you everywhere I go."

She pushed her coffee cup aside and threw up her hands. "Fine. I'll move in with you, but I'm not going to like it."

Drey motioned for the waitress to bring him another beer while thinking he probably wouldn't like it a whole hell of a lot either.

A few minutes later Charlene walked into her apartment with Drey following behind. "It'll take me but a minute to pack," she said over her shoulder as she kept moving toward her bedroom. When he didn't say anything she stopped and turned around and was hit with a multitude of sensations, swift and fierce, when she saw him leaning against her closed door staring. "What are you staring at?"

He met her gaze. "You. But more specifically the shape of your backside. I like it."

She crossed her arms over her chest. "Not that I care whether you like it or not, but I prefer you not to think of me as only a sex object."

"I don't. You're smart, intelligent and attractive. You also have a body that I find fascinating. Why were you hiding it behind lab coats?"

"Everyone who works in the coroner's office wears lab coats. At home I dress like any normal person. Until last night you had no reason to see me anywhere other than where I work."

Drey lifted his broad shoulders in a shrug. "You're right, of course," he said smoothly. "Now I'll be seeing you all the time."

"If you're going to have a problem with it, please let me know now. I won't move in with you only to feel uncomfortable being around you," she said firmly.

"I won't have a problem with it and you'll have no reason to feel uncomfortable. I told you where we stood. However, as a man I find it hard to ignore some things when it comes to a woman, but I'll cope."

Charlene saw the way he was looking at her and wasn't so sure. Her uncertainty blended with apprehension.

"I told you nothing will happen between us until you want it," he tried assuring her. "But I can promise you that when that time comes I will be ready."

His statement caused a deep stirring in her stomach and she fought the sensations, despising her traitorous body for responding to his words, his promise. She sighed deeply. He wouldn't be making such promises if he had any idea just how limited her experience was.

Instead of saying anything else to him she turned and went into her bedroom, closing the door behind her.

Drey watched her departure and shook his head, refusing to give in to the lust that tried over-taking his mind and body whenever he was around Charlene. That wasn't good, especially since she would be moving in with him. Like he'd told her, nothing would happen unless she issued an invitation and with her stubbornness, he couldn't see that happening any time soon, which was fine with him since he needed to get his mind back on the investigation.

That meant he needed to talk with his mother.

Taking his cell phone out of his pocket, he punched in his mother's business number. A few minutes later he hung up after being told she had left work early that day. He tried her cell number but she didn't answer there either. He decided not to leave a message. Maybe he'd make it his business to drop by his mother's home tomorrow so they could continue the discussion they'd started a few days ago. He wanted the whole story about Harmon and he intended to get it. He refused to let his mother evade him any longer.

Flexing his muscles to ease away the frustration he felt, he walked over to the window and glanced out just in time to see a white Maxima slow up when it passed by Charlene's condo. He stood and watched, making sure he wasn't seen. His features hardened. Had Charlene's boss put out the word on her already? The car momentarily came to a stop before moving on.

"I'm through packing."

Charlene's voice got his attention. He turned around and saw the overnight bag she held in her hand. "Am I to assume you were able to fit all your belongings in that?" he asked, pointing at her bag.

"No, of course this isn't everything. I'll come back for the rest at some other time."

"No, you can't."

Before she could gear up to give him the retort that would probably blaze his ears, he asked, "What kind of car does your boss have?"

He could tell his question threw her for a loop. "What?"

"I asked what kind of car your boss has."

Her brows arched as she considered his question. "A white Maxima. Why?"

Drey glanced toward the window. "He just drove by. It's my guess he needed to see if you heeded his warning or not, so it's a good thing we came in my car."

He looked back at her. "Chances are he was probably concerned as to whether he would have to report to someone what you may or may not know and he was trying to avoid doing that."

He saw the tenseness that filled her eyes and knew it was time for her to realize just what kind of dangerous situation she was in. "I know you don't want to leave here, Charlene, but I hope now you see that until I discover who's behind those deaths that you're not safe staying here."

She jutted out her chin. "But what if you never find those responsible? What if—"

"What if you show a little confidence in my abilities?" he interrupted by saying in a harsh tone. "Now please go back in there and pack like you were supposed to be doing in the first place."

The silence as well as the tension in the room reached a monumental peak. Drey very seldom got angry, but Charlene was trying his patience big time. Between her and his mother he had been encountering more emotions in one week than in all the years since he was a teenager and his father had died.

Her dark eyes blazed at him. "Fine. I'll do as you've requested."

About time. Instead of saying what he felt or the scorching comment that was on the tip of his tongue, he nodded and then walked back over to the window, fully aware of the moment she left the room.

Chapter 6

Mumbling under her breath, Charlene began throwing things out of the drawers and onto her bed. Drey had a way of using a tone of command even when he assumed that he was speaking nicely. He had a lot to learn to master the use of persuasive language.

Jeez! She couldn't believe this was happening to her. First she was forced to take time off her job and now she was forced to move in with the person responsible for her predicament. She was trying hard to control her anger, but it wasn't working.

The only thing working was the achy feeling in the pit of her stomach at the mere thought of sharing living quarters with Drey. Remembering all the words she had spouted earlier, she felt trapped between a rock and a hard place with no way out. More to the point, she felt as if she would be held hostage. Just the thought that he would have his eyes on her, watching her practically every minute, her every move, didn't sit well with her. For crying out loud, it was the most ridiculous thing she'd ever heard…but at the same time just as he'd said, it was the only way to ensure her safety.

Not liking the very thought of that, she crossed the room to her closet and flung open the door. She didn't want to become indebted to Drey for making her the object of his protection, and at the moment she preferred not to feel she owed him anything.

She went through her clothes, wondering what she should take and what she should leave behind. Certain outfits were a must, but then a few others she felt would send Drey the wrong message and she refused to give the man any more ideas than he already had.

A short while later she had loaded everything

she felt she needed into the luggage she had taken from underneath her bed. Suddenly everything inside her tensed and she glanced around to find Drey standing casually in the doorway.

She inhaled sharply, trying not to stare. Today he wore boots, a pair of jeans and a blue chambray shirt. His height made him appear taller and his stance exuded lethal sexuality in a way that was heating up the blood flowing through her veins. Earlier at the café when she had looked up and watched him approach her table in a walk that was sexier than anything she'd ever seen, she had been forced to expel a calming breath. She talked with surefire confidence around him when deep down she knew she'd have to watch her guard or she would be in trouble. The last thing she needed was to live under the same roof with a man who got on her nerves one minute and had the ability to cause havoc with her hormones the next.

"Need help with anything?"

Charlene inhaled deeply, forcing herself to relax, but found doing so rather difficult. His deep voice felt like silk across her skin, caressing her in places she rather not think about. She was beginning to regard him as a risk she should avoid taking. The man had all but stated—and in explicit terms—what he would do to her if given the chance. But she was determined to make sure nothing happened between them, no matter how tempting the thought. "No, thank you, I can handle things myself."

He straightened away from the doorway to move into the room, coming to a stop by the bed. "I'm not so sure that you can. This luggage is a lot bigger than you are."

"I can handle it," she said, zipping up the luggage while struggling to keep calm. Sexual chemistry was becoming a constant between them and she wished it would go away, find someone else to torture.

She reached to pull the luggage off the bed the same time Drey did. Their hands touched and she jerked back as if she had been scorched.

"Drey," she said brusquely. "I told you I could handle it."

"Yes, and I recall saying the luggage was as big as you are and that I would help."

Charlene took a step back away from the bed. "Then by all means, flex your muscles. After all,

I'm just a weak woman who can't do anything for herself."

Drey cocked his head and stared at her with a bit of hardness in his eyes. "What you can do is remove that chip off your shoulder, Charlene."

With his statement her anger lost some of its punch. Was she acting as if she had a chip on her shoulder? If so, she had good reason. She gave a breathy yet sarcastic laugh. "How would you like to be in my predicament?" she asked in a flippant tone.

"Frankly, I wouldn't. But I certainly wouldn't bite the hand that's trying to help me every chance I got."

She finger-combed a lock of hair behind her ear and exhaled, putting up a good fight between being defiant and being reasonable. "Look, my day hasn't gone like I had hoped and I'm in a bad mood. Sorry if it seems that I'm taking it out on you, but being forced to leave my home wasn't what I'd counted on when I woke up this morning."

"And I understand and feel somewhat responsible for that. However, our situation is as it is, and to make the most of it I think we need to at least try to work together and not snap at each other at every opportune moment. Don't you agree?"

Grudgingly, she said, "Yes."

"Okay then, I believe this calls for a truce," he said, offering his hand to her.

Charlene paused a moment before accepting his hand. The moment she touched it she knew why she had resisted doing so. Instead of shaking her hand and releasing it, he held on to it, closed his fingers around hers.

"I told you last night that you had pretty hands. What I didn't get the chance to say is that there's something about your hand that I find irresistible."

He turned her hand over and then fingered the lines in the palm, studying them as he did so. She tried to ignore the sensations that raced through her with his touch and was tempted to pull her hand from his as she had done last night.

Moments later, he raised his head and met her gaze. "Do you know anything about Chinese palm reading?"

"No, do you?" She tried not to respond smartly, but it came out that way anyway.

But for once he didn't seem to mind her tone

and actually chuckled. "Yes. My mother is half Chinese and as a child I got a chance to visit her family in China for an entire summer. My great-grandmother explained that Chinese palm reading is an ancient art passed down from generation to generation. By reading the lines in a person's hands a skilled palm reader can find out everything there is to know about that person."

"So now you're claiming to be a palm reader, Drey?"

"Somewhat."

He sounded serious and she wasn't sure whether to believe him or not, but she decided to call his bluff. "Okay, what does mine say?"

He closed her hand before releasing it. "I'll make a point to tell you one day."

She lifted a brow, wondering if he'd seen something she should be concerned with, then decided he was probably pulling her leg. "Whatever," she said, rubbing her hands together, trying to rid them of the feel of his touch that seemed to linger and wouldn't go away. "I'm ready to leave if you are."

"Okay."

She then watched as he effortlessly lifted the luggage off the bed, and followed him from her bedroom. When they got to the living room he glanced over at her phone. "You might want to leave a message giving the impression you've left town for a while, just in case anyone is curious enough to check."

Knowing he had a point, she quickly crossed the room and within minutes had done what he had suggested. When she returned to where he stood and glanced up at him, she noticed how his eyes had darkened and were filled with an intensity she had immediately associated with him. *Desire.* And she knew the cause of it. He had watched her walk across the room, checking out her rear end with every step she had taken.

She frowned. "You have a problem," she said, knowing he was aware of what she was talking about.

A wry smile curved his lips. "Some men are leg men, others prefer breasts. Personally, I have a fetish for the hind part." And without waiting for her to comment, he walked off.

Charlene watched him go, thinking since fanny-watching seemed to be fair play, she might as well check out his. *Umm, not bad.* In fact she thought he had a real nice-looking tush.

He stopped when he got to the door and looked over his shoulder at her and gave her a smile that only heightened his sexiness. "Like what you see?"

She could lie and say no, she didn't like it, but decided this was one time she would be honest with him…up to a point. "Possibly."

He chuckled. "Fair enough. And to answer your question from earlier, about what I see in your hands…. One thing I found interesting is the fact you are a very passionate woman."

A passionate woman? Who was he kidding? "If you say so."

"I do and one day I intend to prove it to you."

His ultimate goal, Drey thought, was to finish the investigation and make it possible for Charlene to return to her home—but not before he had taken her to bed. He glanced over at her, saw the way she avoided looking at him by keeping her eyes focused on the scenery outside the car window, and wondered what she would think of his plans if she knew them, especially the part about him sleeping with her.

He didn't mind letting her know that he wanted her. It would be hard keeping something like that a secret anyway while they lived under the same roof. But she didn't have to know she was at the top of his to-do list. He had given her fair warning, but for some reason she didn't believe him.

He'd even left it up to her as to how she would handle him and the situation. However, for some reason she assumed she could keep sexual urges, tension and good old chemistry at bay by doing nothing and pretending they didn't exist between them. What planet had she been living on most of her life?

Any hot-blooded adult knew the best way to handle red-hot lust was to work the person out of your system and move on, which was something he intended to do. He could handle her bouts of anger just as he would be able to handle whatever degree of desire she had the ability to whip up within him. As he had told her earlier, she was a passionate woman. Not only could he feel it in her hands, but he had tasted it in her kiss and he could even pick it up in her scent. The way he was doing now.

"Tell me about your family, Drey."

Her words cut into his thoughts and he glanced over at her. For reasons unbeknownst to her, his family was the last thing he wanted to talk about.

He brought his car to a stop at a traffic light, inclined his head and said, "How about telling me about yours?"

From her expression he could tell she hadn't expected that. It was obvious she preferred not talking about her family, but since she had been the one to bring up the subject, he figured that eventually she would respond.

It took her a while and then she said, "My parents divorced when I was ten. I took their divorce hard until I realized they were happier living apart. Neither of them liked the idea of being single so they remarried quickly, and before you ask, no, not to each other. My mother is into her fourth marriage and Dad is involved with wife number three. I'm the only child they had together, but I have a number of stepsisters and stepbrothers."

"And do you get along with them?"

She shrugged. "Most of the time. But then there have been occasions when they avoid me like I avoid them."

She glanced over at him when he stopped the car to another traffic light. "What about you? Are you an only child?"

He thought about her question and decided to answer it the way he felt best. "Yes. My father was a cop. He died when I was in my teens. My mom is still alive and in good health."

"How did your dad die?"

"In the line of duty," he said, remembering that day so clearly in his mind.

"Sorry."

"So was I," he said automatically, noticing how his voice had lowered, how he still felt pain after all these years. And then he added, "We were close." After saying those words he wondered why he had told her that. His relationship with his father had never been up for discussion with anyone other than his mother.

"Is that why you became a policeman?"

"Pretty much," he said evenly, knowing that *had* been the reason. "Dad was a good cop and I wanted to be like him. I was on the streets a few years before I decided I didn't want to put up with all the beauracacy that went along with it."

"So you became a private investigator instead?"

"Yes." He remembered how much Harmon had played into that decision and the support he had given him. "And I've never regretted it, although the first few years were hard. Clients were scarce." He chuckled. "And it took me forever to solve my first case."

"Tell me about it."

Drey glanced over at her. She seemed truly interested and wasn't just asking for conversation's sake. He didn't say anything for several long moments and then he began talking and was surprised how easy it was to open up to her. He remembered the case as if it were yesterday when Sharon Mosley had shown up at his office and hired him to get the goods on her cheating husband. It hadn't been the type of case he'd wanted starting out, but it had eventually paid the bills. When it had come to adultery, Kent Mosley had covered his tracks well, refusing to let his wife of thirty-something years get anything on him that could entice her to take him to the cleaner's. His luck finally ran out when Drey captured on film the man making out with the wife of one of his business associates.

Over the next few minutes Drey talked and Charlene listened; she even asked him a few questions every now and then. He wasn't surprised by her intelligence or how quick she was in figuring out things. Pretty soon they were pulling back into the parking lot of the café where they had left her car.

"You can follow me back to my place. It's not far from here," he said, bringing his car to a stop next to hers.

"Okay," she said, unsnapping her seat belt and turning to open the door.

Drey glanced in his rearview mirror, something he'd done several times to make sure they hadn't been followed. He glanced back at her in time to see one smooth thigh when she descended from the vehicle. And again when she got into her car. His mouth hardened. That hadn't been what his already horny body needed to see.

He only began driving away when he was certain she was following him.

It was then that he decided to try contacting his mother again. Pulling his cell from off his belt, he flipped it open to punch in his mother's number only to be met with the answering machine again. This time he left a message.

"Mom, this is Drey. We need to talk. I would appreciate if you'd call me later."

He hung up the line wondering how soon she

would contact him and whether he was ready to hear what else she had to say.

Charlene was quiet as she listened to the soft jazz sound on the radio while following behind Drey. She couldn't help wondering what she had gotten herself into. She knew moving in with him on a temporary basis was the smart thing to do, but that didn't mean she had to like it.

He had surprised her when he had opened up and told her about the first case he had taken on as a private investigator. She had found it interesting, but more than anything she had admired his diligence in solving the case. She figured getting him to talk would ease some of the heated tension between them. It had for a while, but she had felt his eyes watching her every movement when she had gotten out of his car. It was if he'd been undressing her with his gaze. How in the world would they manage to live under the same roof? She had never felt this desired by a man in her entire life.

Of course she knew it was a passing fancy for Drey. She couldn't allow herself to get caught up in what was probably one of his testosterone moments.

She followed his car into a gated community and as she pulled in directly behind him, she glanced around at the large town houses that made her place look like a dollhouse.

A smile touched her lips. Drey's first case might have been the pits, but evidently he had recovered nicely. She nearly jumped when her cell phone went off in her purse and she eased it out and flipped it open after seeing the caller was her mother. "Yes, Mom?"

"I called your house and there's a message on your phone indicating you're out of town. You didn't mention coming to Florida, so does that mean you're visiting your father?"

Charlene rolled her eyes. Another issue she had with her parents was their constant competitive nature where she was concerned. Her mother did not like her father's third wife and wanted to make sure Charlene didn't like her either. "No, Mom, I'm not visiting Dad. I just need to get away for a while."

"Why?" her mother demanded, as if she had every right to know.

"Things are crazy at work," she said truthfully. "So I thought I'd take a few days off, go somewhere and enjoy myself." *Enjoy herself?* She had to be kidding. She watched as Drey parked his car and got out, saw how nicely his jeans covered his tush and knew she *was* kidding. Inexplicably, a heated sensation flowed through her.

"Better do it now before you stress yourself out," her mother said. "Stress isn't good. That's why I stopped working."

Charlene frowned. She'd never known her mother to work outside the home. At fifty, Nina was still a beautiful woman and would be a trophy on any man's arms. When Charlene saw that Drey had turned and was waiting for her to get out of the car, she quickly said, "Okay, Mom, I need to go. Someone is waiting for me."

"It's a man, right? Tell me that you got away with a man."

Charlene's mouth tightened. Why was her mother so obsessed with her finding a man? "Yes, Mom, I'm spending some time with a man," she said, giving in to what she knew her mother wanted to hear. "I'll touch base with you when I return."

"You haven't said where you are."

No, intentionally, she hadn't. Charlene glanced around and noticed the name of the community and saw the huge water fountain close by as well as the well-tended landscaped yard. "It's called Kindle Wood Lakes and it's near the water." Okay, so she was stretching the truth a little bit.

"Sounds like a real nice resort. Have fun and don't make any babies until after the wedding."

"Mom!"

"Don't Mom me since I was young once. Besides, I'd like to have a son-in-law while I'm young enough to appreciate him."

Yes, Charlene thought, she knew that, had accepted it and most of the time just plain ignored it. "Goodbye, Mom."

"Goodbye, sweetheart."

Drey leaned back against his car and watched Charlene get out of hers with a frown on her face. He had seen her cell phone plastered to her ear and had wondered who she was talking to. Whomever it was evidently had gotten her a little annoyed. Had her boss tried contacting her? His protective instinct automatically kicked in, and when she reached his side he asked, "Are you okay?"

She glanced around, looking everywhere else

but at him when she said, "Yes, I'm fine. I just finished talking to my mother."

He knew damned good and well he shouldn't care one iota about her relationship with her mother but heard himself remarking anyway, "You were frowning."

She looked at him. "I usually do whenever I talk to either of my parents. Sometimes they forget our agreement."

"Which is?"

He would not have been surprised if she had told him it was none of his business, because truly it wasn't. So she sort of stunned him when she answered, "Considering their numerous marriages, they promised me on my twenty-first birthday that they would stay out of my business if I stayed out of theirs. Staying out of theirs is a piece of cake, but they still find it a challenge to stay out of mine. Especially Mom. She's constantly reminding me that my biological clock is ticking and wants me to do something about it."

Drey laughed. "So in other words, she wants grandchildren." He'd heard the same request a number of times from his own mother.

"She wants me to find a husband before I start

populating the earth and gets quite annoyed with me by my lack of interest."

Lack of interest? He couldn't help but remember she had gotten quite annoyed with him last night when he'd asked why she didn't have a date.

"My mother thinks we're having an affair."

"Excuse me?" Staring down at her, he could clearly see the red highlights in her hair, although she was wearing her hair pinned up in a knot on her head. He preferred seeing it down the way she'd worn it last night.

"She called my apartment and got my message about me going out of town. I couldn't tell her the truth, so I fabricated a story for her that included a trip away for a few days, and of course she assumed it was with a man."

"And she's okay with that?"

"Overjoyed, actually. Like I said earlier, she thinks my biological clock is ticking."

He watched as she glanced around again. "Nice community. Have you lived here long?" she asked.

"A couple of years." He pushed away from his car. "Are you ready to go in? I can come back for your stuff later."

He then smiled when he saw the look of apprehension on her face. "Will it make you feel better if I promise not to jump your bones as soon as I get you over the threshold?"

She narrowed her gaze. "I'm glad one of us finds all of this amusing."

Drey held up both hands in a defensive pose. "Hey, don't get uptight on me. I don't find the thought of your life being in danger amusing. What I do find amusing is your reaction to the idea of living with me for a while. I take it you've never shared quarters with a man."

"Of course not!"

"Any reason why?"

She didn't answer immediately, so he figured she was thinking about his question. "I'm nitpicky."

"So am I, but I have a feeling we'll get along just nicely."

She opened her mouth as if to say something, then quickly closed it, leaving him wondering just what was on her mind. "Get it out, Charlie. Say whatever you want."

Her eyes narrowed at him and then she asked, "Just in case one of your lady friends shows up and wonders who I am, what should I tell them?"

"I doubt that will happen, but if it does the simple thing is to tell them you're my girl."

She shook her head. "No way would I lie like that."

"Then if it will make you feel better, tell them you're my long lost sister, although I doubt they'll believe you."

Determined to end this topic of conversation before he would be forced to tell her that she would be wearing the title of "Drey's lover" before long, he began moving toward his front door. She walked at a leisurely pace next to him and for the first time in a long while he liked the thought of a woman by his side.

Another thought that flashed through his mind was that Charlene was used to handling dead bodies. There was nothing dead about him and soon enough she would discover how it was to handle a living, breathing, hot-blooded man.

Chapter 7

Charlene froze the moment she stepped over the threshold in Drey's home, finding his taste in furniture and decorating utterly exquisite. Her gaze was immediately drawn to the numerous selections of Asian artwork he had on his walls. Even from a distance she found them intriguingly unusual and definitely exotic.

She crossed the room, immediately smitten with one painting in particular. She couldn't help but study the richness of the colors the artist had used as well as the selection of a mahogany-trimmed leather frame. It was a painting of a beautiful Asian woman, drenched in a multicolored robe as she walked through a flower garden with a shimmering pond in the background. The expression on the woman's face was both exotic and erotic.

"I see you like this one," she heard Drey say, coming up behind her. She tensed, immediately feeling his heat, which made her totally aware of his masculinity. Those thoughts made her even more determined to keep a tight rein on her control as well as her common senses while around him.

"Yes, it's different, although I'm surprised to find such a painting in your living room. It seems more fitted for the bedroom."

Drey chuckled. "Yeah, probably, but I prefer to have it out here."

"She's beautiful."

"Thanks. When I see her I'll tell her you said that."

Charlene spun around, her eyebrows arched. "You know her?"

"Yes. I know her. That's my mother."

Charlene blinked before turning back at the picture, amazed. "Your mother?"

Drey smiled. "Yes. She was only twenty-three when it was painted and she gave it to my father as a wedding gift." He didn't say anything for a while, then added, "I recall it was one of Dad's most prized possessions."

Charlene could clearly see why. As she'd said earlier, the woman was beautiful. Although he had told her about his parents, he hadn't said a lot about his mother, other than the state of her health. He'd mostly spoken of his father. She wondered if his relationship with his mother was strained for some reason.

"Come on, I'll give you a tour of the place and then I'll show you to the room that you'll be using while you're here."

The tour made her realize even more just what a beautiful home Drey had. His kitchen, with stainless steel appliances, was to die for, large and spacious. He told her he enjoyed cooking and spent a lot of time in the kitchen. She could tell just from looking around that like her, he was neat and tidy and liked nice things. She could also tell that his tastes included the exotic and she figured they were mainly because of his background.

He worked from his home, so the room he

considered as his office reflected such. It wasn't cluttered although a number of files were open on his desk. He told her that he had a woman come in a couple of days a week to file and manage the books.

The guest room was neatly decorated although he told her that in the three years he lived there she was officially his first guest. The view out of her bedroom window faced the lake. The only problem she had was the proximity of her bedroom to his. It was directly across the hall.

Overall, she liked the layout of his home. It was rather spacious for one person, but he indicated he didn't like the feeling of being cramped.

He had just placed her luggage on the bed when his cell phone rang. He pulled it out of his pocket, glanced at who was calling and then flipped it open. "Yes, Mom?"

A few moments later he said. "Good. I'm on my way."

He glanced over at Charlene as he put his cell phone back in his pocket. "I need to go visit with my mother for a while. Will you be okay here while I'm gone?"

She waved off his question. "Of course. After

I unpack I intend to sit outside on the patio. "You have a beautiful view."

"Thanks."

She studied his features, saw the dark look in his eyes and the way his nostrils flared. He was staring at her and the look at that moment was so blatantly sexual, she felt chills run up and down her spine at the same time blood raced through her veins.

"If you get hungry before I return, I have a loaded refrigerator."

She straightened her shoulders. "Thanks."

He suddenly took a step forward and on instinct she took one back, but not quick enough to stop him from reaching out and letting his fingers gently grab her wrist to bring her close to him. "Where do you think you're going?" he asked in a husky tone.

She stood close to him. More than ever she could feel his heat. Standing this close was causing all types of emotions to bombard her inner being. She tilted up her head and met his gaze. "I was trying to get out of your way," she said, trying not to look into the darkness of his eyes. "I'm not here for this, Drey."

A smile touched his lips. "Here for what?"

"To be a live-in woman who is available for you."

He didn't say anything, but she could tell her comment had him thinking and she had a feeling whatever it was, wasn't to her advantage. "I really hadn't thought of you as such, but now that you mention it, Charlie…"

She tried pulling her arm away; instead he pulled her closer with his full concentration on her mouth. "Don't get irritated with me, but before I leave there is something I need from you," he said in a deep, throaty voice.

She gave him a quelling look. Her chin went up. "There is nothing that you could possibly need from me."

"Want to bet?" He released her arm and reached up and let the tip of his finger caress her lips, as if he was fascinated with their shape. Without his hold she had the perfect opportunity to bolt, but she found herself rooted to the spot, held prisoner by the heated look in his eyes.

Looking down at her, he said in a whispered tone, "The shape of your mouth fascinates me."

It was on the tip of her tongue to say the shape of his mouth fascinated her, as well. But she didn't.

Instead she continued to watch him while intense heat seemed to flood every part of her body.

"I want to kiss you, Charlene."

His words had her swallowing deeply. They had every nerve ending in her body on fire. "If I let you kiss me, it will give you the wrong idea."

She watched the corners of his lips tilt into a smile that nearly took her breath away. "Or it could give me the right one," he answered.

She signed deeply. "You mother is waiting," she said, deciding to remind him he had more pressing matters to take care of.

He still didn't move. "Drey," she said softly. "I think that "

"Shh, don't think at all for a second," he whispered, removing his hand from her face to place it at her waist. "Just close your eyes and experience the taste."

He leaned in closer and lowered his head. His breath felt hot and wet against her lips, "Will you do that for me, Charlene?"

There was something in the way he asked that touched a part deep within her, persuading her to give in to his request. And just that easily she closed her eyes and within seconds, she felt his mouth on hers as he began kissing her in a slow, yet deep connection that devoured her with each stroke of his tongue.

It was like taking a sip of a bubbly drink in a highly charged room. That was the only way she could describe the feelings that were overtaking her senses. Just once she didn't want to think that this was a kiss with a purpose or one that wasn't meant to happen. Instead she catered to needs she'd never encountered before and let herself be swept away by a multitude of feelings. Grudgingly she conceded that she wanted to indulge in this type of kiss as much as he did. It was a stimulant to her senses, a boost to her hormones and a must-do to her brain cells.

The kiss was everything it should be and more. And it reminded her of what she'd been missing out on for a long time. A life filled with long hours at work without any type of social life had led her to this. She didn't understand why they were drawn to each other, but she couldn't deny they were and had been from the first, although they'd tried downplaying it.

The kiss turned greedy, almost shamefully erotic, as he shifted his stance to take as much of her mouth as he could. His arms tightened around her like a band of steel and she was pulled even closer into his tight embrace.

For a split second she came close to moaning deep in her throat, but held it back and shivered under the impact of what he was doing to her mouth. She felt the physical evidence of his desire pressed against the apex of her thighs. It both frightened her and elated her that she had the ability to elevate his desire and bring him to this point.

He slowly released her mouth but not before taking his tongue and licking her lips from corner to corner, then sliding it back into her mouth for one final intense mating. She clung to his tongue with her own, feeling the strength in it, while her body quivered in the rush of sensations passing through her.

The moan she couldn't hold back any longer came out in a soft whimper, and at the same time her knees weakened under such intense passion. When it came to the art of kissing, Drey was an expert. He had the ability to take it to a level she had never experienced until now.

He finally pulled back from her mouth and lifted

his head. The dark eyes staring into hers almost made her dizzy and she watched as his eyes lowered from hers to flick over her lips once again.

"I'd better go before I kiss you again," he said in a low, deep voice. "If I keep it up I'll make good my threat."

She swallowed, knowing just what threat he was talking about. The one about kissing her all over. If he did make good his threat, she was doubtful she would be strong enough to resist.

"I'll be back later. Just make yourself at home."

And then he released her and smiled down at her. It wasn't a smile of victory, but one of contentment. She could tell from the expression on his face that he had needed that kiss as much as she had and the enjoyment of it was mutual. That kiss had been the turning point for her and she admitted at that very moment that she wanted to get to know Drey St. John on an even deeper level.

Chapter 8

As much as he wanted to, Drey could not dismiss
the impact on his senses of the kiss he had shared
with Charlene. He felt a tight squeeze in his chest
when he thought about what she was doing to
him. And he didn't like it one bit.

He hadn't been able to walk out the door quick
enough. Temptation had been nipping at his heels
to go back inside of his home and pull her into his
arms for another round. It had taken everything he
had to get into his car and drive away. Even now he
was fighting the urge to turn around and go back.

When was the last time a woman had taken such a toll on his libdo? Probably never. He had invited Charlene into his home, totally unprepared for the degree of attraction he had for her. He'd been very much aware that he wanted her before, but what he hadn't been prepared for was his lack of control around her, where at every opportune moment he wanted to drag her into his arms and kiss her senseless. He was not one who easily succumbed to passion, but he had today. If he could have had his way he would still be kissing her.

No, he would have escalated things to another level by now. At some point she would have made it to his bed and he would be inside her this very moment. The mere thought had intense desire flooding all parts of him, especially one that was destined to explode if it didn't get some relief.

It didn't take long to reach his mother's house, and for a few highly charged moments he remained in his car, trying to bring a semblance of control back to his body. After taking several deep breaths he cut off the ignition and calmed the wild flutterings in his stomach.

He had an investigation to complete and he could not lose sight of the fact that somehow his own mother might be involved. The last time he had been here she had dropped a bombshell that had rocked his entire world. And now he wanted to know everything, hear the entire story. He wanted her to explain just how thirty-three years ago she had gotten involved with a married man.

Drey had done the math. Harmon Braddock had been married at the time he and Daiyu had been involved. For the life of him, Drey could not picture his mother as a home-wrecker. His parents had shared a beautiful marriage. She had been completely dedicated to his father. She had taken Ronald St. John's death just as hard as he had and over the years since then, she had not gotten serious with another man, although he had known there had been a few who'd been interested. Just as Charlene had stated, his mother had been and still was a very beautiful woman.

He glanced around. The approach of winter hadn't stopped his mother from spending time outdoors in her garden. The last time he was here the plants had looked a little sickly. Now they looked alive and vibrant, which meant although his mother had avoided him for the past few days, she had managed to tend to her garden.

He thought about why he was here. It seemed the one woman he loved most in the world had been keeping secrets. Secrets he was slowly unraveling.

Getting out of the car, he moved up the walkway toward the Cape Cod-style house as his mind filled with memories of other times he'd taken this same path. It wasn't unusual for him to drop by on occasion to see how she was doing or to see if she needed his assistance. His mother was an independent woman and although he always offered his services, she preferred doing things for herself. He'd always admired that about her.

Taking the keys out of his back pocket, he let himself in as he'd always done. At any other time his mother would be at work, but she had called and said she wanted to finish their conversation, which meant she'd be waiting for him to arrive.

He walked through the house and went straight to the kitchen. He found her there, sitting at the table with her hands crossed on top of it. Her long dark hair hung past her shoulders, and like his, her eyes were dark and slanted over high cheekbones and a rounded face. She was an Asian beauty who looked like thirty-five instead of fifty-five.

"I heard your car pull up," she said, tilting her head back to look up at him.

He crossed the room to give her a peck on the cheek. "Hi, Mom."

"Drey. If you're hungry, I can make—"

"No, I'm not hungry," he said, taking the chair across from her and thinking that he didn't want to put anything in his mouth just yet that would diminish Charlene's taste. He wanted to savor it for a little while longer.

He glanced around the kitchen and saw all the pots on the stove. "You've been busy," he said, when it was quite obvious that she had been. She once told him that she did a lot of cooking when she was nervous about something.

Evidently that was the case now.

Deciding to get to the heart of the matter, he said, "Mom, the last time we talked you shared some things with me. However, I left before you could finish telling me everything."

He knew that was putting it mildly since he hadn't given her a chance to tell him anything else. The dam had burst once she had admitted that

Harmon Braddock was his father. It was pretty obvious how upset he'd gotten that day upon hearing it. He had walked out angry, mad at the world, especially at her for not being truthful with him for all those years.

"All right, where do you want me to start?" she asked, her voice low and shaky.

"From the beginning. I want to know how you and Harmon Braddock met."

She said nothing for a moment while studying the teacup. Then she began speaking. "As you know I came to this country at the age of twenty as part of an international exchange program with Stewart Industries."

"Yes." He had heard that part before a number of times.

"Well, one week I got to attend a conference for Stewart Industries. Harmon was staying at the same hotel. We met at the hotel bar and I thought he was the most handsome and charismatic man I'd ever met. That week we became involved in an intense affair."

"Did you know he was married?"

She met his gaze. "No, I didn't know, at least not at first. Apparently he and his wife were having marital problems. However, once he told me the truth, that he was a married man, I threatened to break things off."

"But you didn't." He wished his words hadn't sounded so accusatory.

"No, I didn't break it off. I was convinced that he would leave his wife to be with me."

"Did he tell you that he would?"

She shook her head. "No. I just assumed that he would. I was young, inexperienced and in love and I thought that he would leave his wife because he was unhappy at the time. He didn't. After about a few months he ended things between us, and said he and his wife were going to try and make their marriage work." His mother paused for a moment before adding. "Not long after that I discovered I was pregnant."

Now it was Drey's time to pause to absorb everything his mother had said thus far. Then he asked, "Did you tell him you were pregnant?"

"No. I was scared to tell him so I kept it a secret. It was during that time, not too long after me and Harmon broke up, that I met Ronald. He wanted to take me out and I told him up front that I was pregnant, but that didn't matter to him.

Ronald had fallen in love with me and wanted to make my child his own."

Drey didn't say anything but he sat there, looking out the window at her flower garden. His gaze returned to hers when he asked, "But Braddock eventually found out about me." He figured as much since the man had sought him out.

"Yes. I ran into him one day and he saw me pregnant. He put two and two together and realized the child was his. I was still hoping he wanted me and actually told him that I would end my relationship with Ronald if he left his wife. He said it was too late. His wife was pregnant and he was worried about the potential damage it would do to her if she were to find out. So we decided to cut our losses and move on, go our separate ways. I married your father and worked hard to make him a wonderful wife."

Drey held back his brutal retort that she hadn't given his father anything less than what he'd deserved. Ronald St. John had been a wonderful husband and father. Had his mother only shared part of her love with him? Had the other been for another man who had used her?

"But Harmon always kept up with what was

going on with you, Drey," his mother said, breaking into his thoughts.

"And how would you know that?" he asked, wondering if this was where she would admit that she and Harmon had picked back up their affair after she'd married, and that in doing so, she had been unfaithful to his father.

"Because he told me he always would," she replied. "After Ronald was killed and he saw how hard you were struggling with his death, he reentered the picture to be there for you and eventually became your mentor. I wasn't happy about it, but as long as he kept his agreement and didn't tell you he was your biological father, I told him that I wouldn't stop him from building a relationship with you. And he wanted that, Drey. Harmon wanted to get close to you. He felt being your mentor, being there when and if you ever needed him, would be the only way he could have anything close to a father/son relationship with you."

Drey inhaled deeply, trying to keep his control from snapping. He felt as though his entire life hadn't been anything but a lie. He'd always liked the congressman, but now he wasn't sure how he should feel about him. The man had totally used his mother when it had been convenient, and then walked out of her life, only to return years later when his conscience probably had begun bothering him.

And then Drey thought about his siblings. It had been hard to gaze into Malcolm's face earlier that day without thinking that they were brothers. And how would he deal with Tyson and Shondra when he saw them again? And what about Evelyn, Harmon's widow? How would he deal with her as well? Her husband had been having an affair while she was pregnant with their first child.

However, as far as he was concerned, the person who had suffered the most was Ronald St. John. His father had loved his wife deeply, only to be given part of her love in return. Drey thought of all those years he had allowed Harmon to be his mentor when he had no clue he was the man's son. A part of him felt an outright betrayal to Ronald, the only father he'd ever known.

He pushed back his chair and stood, devastated and unable to hear anything else for now. "Look, Mom, I need to go. I'll talk to you later."

"No, Drey," Daiyu said in a firm tone as she

came to her feet. "I won't let you walk out on me again, and I refuse to let you think I didn't love Ronald, because I did. I grew to love him in a way that I could never love anyone else, including Harmon. Ronald was everything to me like he was everything to you. Your father was my whole world. Even now I miss everything about him. I miss his warm and loving nature, the times we shared together, our special love."

Drey pulled in a deep breath when he heard the sadness in his mother's voice. Then he saw the tears that clung to her lashes. He felt like an ass for making her cry. Gritting his teeth, he moved around the table to pull her small frame into his arms.

"I'm sorry, Mom, I didn't mean to upset you. It's just hard finding out Dad wasn't my father."

His mother pulled back slightly and gazed up at him. "But Ronald *was* your father in every way that counted. He gave you his name and his love. He could not have loved you more if you had been his natural child. He said so many times."

Drey believed her. He also knew talking about his father had taken a toll on her, but there was one other question he needed for her to answer.

He eased her away from him slightly but maintained an arm around her shoulder. "Mom, do you have any idea why Braddock was trying to reach you the night he was killed?"

She shook her head. "No, but he called several times that week before finally getting me. Our conversation was short because he had a call come in on his other line. He said he would call me back but he didn't."

Drey met his other gaze. "Can you think of anything else I need to know?" he asked, knowing the question was still out there as to why Harmon had tried calling his mother that night.

His mother lowered her gaze and pulled completely out of his arms. She went back to the table and sat down in the chair she had vacated earlier. "Yes, there is something."

Drey lifted a brow. "What?"

"Evelyn Braddock came to see me last week."

There was a moment of complete silence, shrouded in tension, when Drey came to sit back down at the table. "For what reason?" He leaned closer to his mother.

Daiyu took a sip of her tea before meeting her son's concerned gaze. "She had heard about

Harmon's calls to Stewart Industries and knew I worked there."

Drey nodded. "Had the two of you met before?"

"Yes, years before. The night he broke things off with me she was with him. I guess it was their way of showing me they had both come to terms with his affair and were working through it."

Drey could only think that at the time meeting her lover's wife had to have been difficult. "What did she say to you last week when she came to visit?"

"She wanted to know about the call Harmon made to me. I told her that I didn't talk to him. I'm not sure whether she believed me. I could tell she was upset to find out that he had tried contacting me after all these years."

Deciding he wanted something to eat after all, Drey went to the counter and helped himself to a plate of cookies while asking, "Do you know of anyone at Stewart Industries that Harmon was interested in?"

"No. However, I do know that Harmon's daughter took a job there a month or so after his death to find out whose number Harmon called.

It's my understanding that she ended up falling in love with Connor Stewart."

Drey also poured a cup of tea. "That's my understanding as well. And they were able to determine the call from Harmon came to you, but no one knows I'm your son."

Daiyu sighed. "Evelyn never knew I was pregnant, so she's unaware that Harmon has another child. Although you know who they are, they don't know you."

Drey intended to keep things that way until he was forced to do otherwise. He wanted to have completed the investigation by then.

"I'm sorry I don't have more to tell you, Drey."

He glanced over his mother and forced a smile. "That's fine. You've told me enough."

Chapter 9

Charlene went inside Drey's home after sitting on the patio for the past hour or so. Although the weather was a little cool, she had enjoyed sitting there watching the ducks play on the water. They appeared not to have a care in the world and she envied them.

Feeling somewhat hungry, she went into the kitchen. She had checked out his refrigerator and pantry earlier and found both places to be well stocked with food. One thing was certain. She wouldn't starve while living with him.

Within minutes she had prepared a sandwich that would make even the people over at the sandwich shop near work jealous.

And speaking of jealous…

She frowned when she remembered the call that had been left on Drey's answering machine. It was from some Karen, who wanted to know if Drey was interested in a fun time, and if so to come over to her place tonight, along with an extra set of clothes to stay for the weekend. The nerve of the hussy!

She turned when she heard the sound of the key in the door and felt a quickening in her chest when Drey walked in. She frowned thinking that this deep attraction for him was not what she wanted. But then she couldn't dismiss memories of the kisses they had shared. Kisses that still had her lips burning in some places.

She could feel her temperature rise when he strode into the kitchen and stood next to her at the counter and stared down at her sandwich. He then looked back at her and smiled. "Hungry?"

She wished he wouldn't smile in a way that made her want to wrap herself around him, cuddle close and hold on to him real tight. His smile always made him look extremely handsome in a totally masculine and sexy sort of way. "What makes you think that?" she asked.

He chuckled. "The size of your sandwich is a dead giveaway. It's enough to feed two people."

She lifted a brow. "Is that a hint that you want half?"

He shook his head. "No, not half. I ate a bunch of cookies over at Mom's. But I'd love to take a bite."

She picked up the sandwich, lifted it up close to his mouth and offered it to him. "Go ahead. I don't mind sharing."

While she held it he took a bite and she got turned on just by watching him chew. It was the methodical, slow movement of his mouth and the way their eyes stayed connected until he had finished. She swallowed, feeling a mass of heat invade her insides.

"It's okay," he said in a husky tone.

She stared at him, feeling her pulse rate increase. "What's okay?"

"The fact that you want me."

He was one arrogant ass, she thought. He was also correct. She wondered how he had known.

Probably from the sound of her breathing. Instead of denying what he'd said, she looked away out his French doors and saw the ducks were still on the pond. She was then reminded of the phone call he had received earlier.

Placing the rest of her sandwich back on the plate, she grabbed her glass of iced tea and sat down at the table before throwing over her shoulder, "Oh yeah, by the way, Karen called."

He stared at her, as if not comprehending. "Karen?"

"Yes. Karen. She's invited you to her house for a sleepover."

"You answered the phone?"

"No, she left a message." And then Charlene added, "I imagine you're sorry that you missed her call."

"Yeah, I'm all broken up about it."

Charlene looked at him, not sure if he was serious or not. She tried not to glare at him when he came over to the table and sat down. He was a free man to do whatever he wanted. "You can call her back. She left her number."

"No need. I know it by heart."

"Figures," she said under her breath.

"Did you say something?"

"No."

He pushed his chair back from the table. "I'll let you eat in peace while I go over some reports."

She wondered if he was really going to go over any report or if he was rushing off to return Karen's call. He glanced at his watch and then asked, "What time do most of the people leave at the coroner's office?"

"Around seven. Why?"

"No reason. I'll check you out later."

She then watched as he quickly walked off toward his office.

As soon as his office door closed behind him, Drey leaned back against it and pulled in a deep breath. Talk about bringing sexy back. Hell, Charlene Anderson took the icing off the cake. What was there about her that made him want to get her naked each and every time he saw her?

When he had walked into his kitchen and seen her standing there at the counter, in the direct path of the sunlight that was streaming in through the window, his heart began beating at a rapid pace. There was something about her standing in his kitchen, as if she had every right to be there, that had actually turned him on big time.

He had never taken a woman on his kitchen counter, but a few minutes ago he had come close to doing so. There was something about Charlene that tempted him to take her on the kitchen counter, the table, the bar stool. She brought out the wild side of him, a side he seldom showed. Maybe the reason was that she seemed to understand absolutely nothing about the opposite sex. For example, for an entire year the two of them had relentlessly bantered back and forth. He had understood why and accepted that the underlying cause was this deep sexual attraction they were trying to fight. For the longest time he felt she hadn't had a clue. She'd never picked up on the fact that he had been sexually attracted to her at all, nor that each and every time he saw her in that lab coat, he had undressed her with his eyes. Nothing had changed. She was no longer wearing her lab coat, but he was still undressing her with his gaze every chance he got. Wondering what she had on underneath her clothing gave him a boner each and every time, which was something else she never even noticed.

Shaking his head, Drey moved away from the door to his desk thinking that it wasn't an easy thing to admit that any one woman could blow your mind. Karen had nothing on her…other than experience. There was something about the way Charlene had returned his kiss the last two times they'd kissed that had made him wonder just how knowledgeable she was in the art of kissing.

She had been reluctant to put her tongue in his mouth until he had grabbed hold of it with his own and began mating with it. That only made him even more curious as to how often she had actually engaged in a French kiss. Would she carry that same level of inexperience into the bedroom?

A man could tell a lot about a woman's experience with a kiss, and right now he would rate Charlene's experience level to a single digit. Not that he was complaining. He had no qualms about showing her what her last lover had evidently failed to do. Meeting a woman who wasn't all that experienced, one he could introduce to new things in the bedroom, was rather refreshing. In fact he looked forward to doing so.

Drey glanced around the room, and not for the first time he admired the setup of his office. Large,

light and airy, because of a huge window that over-
looked the pond, it was the only room in the house
besides the kitchen that didn't have any carpeting.
Instead he had put in hardwood floors that fit in
perfectly with the contemporary office furniture.

Knowing it was time to focus on work, he pulled
a file out of the drawer, thinking that he needed to
see the original autopsy report on Dennis, and if
he could get his hands on that key, it would help
tremendously. With Charlene no longer working at
the coroner's office for the time being, there was
only one way for him to get the items he needed.
Forced entry.

Drey sighed with frustration. If there was another way, he couldn't think of it. In fact he was
having difficulty in computing that Nate Ganders
had changed the autopsy report and that some
members of the police department might be involved. That made him even more determined to
find out the truth. He had a meeting with the Braddocks in a few days and he wanted to be able to
tell them something positive that he'd uncovered.

He wasn't sure just how long he had worked,
going over the documentation he had collected,
reading the police report on Harmon's accident

and studying in detail again all the phone records and information Gloria had shared with him. Suddenly something outside his window caught his attention.

He crossed the room and saw Charlene. She was standing by the edge of the pond, throwing in bread crumbs to the ducks. His gaze focused in on her. She had put on a jacket and had swapped her skirt for a pair of white denim jeans. Not for the first time, and he doubted it would be for the last, he zeroed in on her backside, thinking just how much he liked it, wanting to cover it with his own body, mate with her from that position where he would enter her womanly core from behind. He inhaled a deep, hot breath, again wondering what there was about her that made his thoughts so sexual.

He observed her for a moment longer before deciding that it would be hard to go back to his desk and refocus on his work now that he'd seen her. Making a quick decision, he moved away from the window and grabbed his jacket off the coatrack and headed out of his office to join her at the pond.

Charlene threw bread crumbs out to the ducks while trying to convince herself that it didn't matter one iota to her that Drey was probably in his office talking on the phone to Karen and planning their hot night together. How many men would give up a chance to be with an eager woman? A woman who evidently had a lot of experience.

A woman who still wasn't a virgin.

For once she would like to come across as a woman in the know, and not get all giddy when being exposed to something new. Like the way Drey always kissed her. She'd been kissed before but not the way he did it. He could heighten her senses just with his tongue. She had only read about that type of kiss. It was the kind of kiss that still had heat sizzling inside you long after the contact ended. Amazing.

"The weather has turned rather chilly, hasn't it?"

At the sound of the deep, masculine voice Charlene turned around so quickly she almost lost her balance. She glanced at Drey, who had come to a stop beside her. "I thought you had a lot to do," she said, deciding not to add "with Karen."

"I've taken care of most of what I plan to do today," he said, shifting his gaze from her to the ducks.

"So, what time are you leaving?"

He looked back to her and raised a dark brow. "Am I supposed to be going some place?"

"Yes, I told you that that Karen person called. I heard the message."

He crossed his arms over his chest. "And?"

"And I figured that, like most men, you wouldn't hesitate to take her up on her offer."

A smile that didn't quite reach his eyes appeared on his face. "Well, today you will learn something new."

"Which is?"

"I'm not like most men. And I don't take advantage of every opportunity being offered. Some you learn to stay away from."

"And is Karen one of those opportunities?"

"Afraid so. She's looking for a husband but she won't find one here."

Charlene studied him. "Does that mean you're not looking for a wife?"

"Yes, it means I'm not looking for a wife. Just a temporary bed partner. It's better for me that way. I don't do well with long-term affairs. The short ones work a whole lot better with my lifestyle."

Charlene wondered if he was throwing out hints. If he was, then he was wasting his time.

Once he discovered she was still a virgin, he would hightail it in the opposite direction real quick.

"So, what would you like to do tonight, Charlene?"

She didn't fail to note Drey had said her name with just the right amount of sugarcoating to spike her hormone level up a notch and couldn't help wondering if it was deliberate. A man with as much skill and experience with women as he possessed had to know when he'd hit the jackpot.

She decided to call his bluff to see just how far he would take this and if he was trying to break down her defenses. "I don't know, Drey. What do you have in mind?" she asked in a voice so soft and seductive it didn't sound like her own.

She watched his eyes darken a little and saw the smooth smile that formed on his lips. "Something that might get the both of us in trouble. But I'm willing to take the chance."

Yeah, I bet you are.

"Think you're interested?" he asked her.

Deciding to play along for a while, she said, "Possibly."

His smile widened and he showed beautiful white teeth. "Good." He glanced down at his watch. "You need to go into the house and change into something dark."

Charlene lifted a brow. He said dark but not sexy. Did he have a fetish for dark clothes? "Why do I need to wear something dark?"

"So you can't be seen."

Now she was confused. Why wouldn't he want to see her? She thought naked skin turned most men on. She met his gaze and saw the mischievous glint and wondered...

"Excuse me, are we talking about the same thing?" she decided to ask.

He gave her a half smile. "I don't know. Are we?"

She didn't have time to play guessing games with him. "Am I wrong or did you suggest we do something tonight that might get us into trouble?"

"No, you aren't wrong. I did suggest that." He leaned in closer, so close she could blatantly feel the heat off his body that seemed to suddenly block the cool air from coming her way. What other reason would her body suddenly feel as if it were burning up inside?

"And I'm curious to know what you thought I was referring to," he said, leaning in even closer.

She was tempted to take a step back, but a part of her refused to do so, afraid if she moved even an inch all those vibrations that were slowly thrumming through her body would get even stronger.

"No, you go first," she said, nervously licking her lips and watching his gaze follow the movement of her tongue. "Tell me what you were talking about."

He reached out and placed his hands at her waist and her body immediately reacted, shooting sparks of fire to every nerve ending. "Okay, what I was talking about us doing tonight, where we might get into trouble, is…"

"Yes?" she asked softly, curiosity eating away at her, especially in some very sensitive places.

"Breaking into the coroner's office to find your boss's original autopsy report on Dennis as well as that key."

"What!" She would have jumped back in shock, but the moment her mouth opened to exclaim that one word, he was right there on it. And that was the last part of their conversation that she remembered.

Chapter 10

She moaned.

The sound made Drey delve into her mouth that much deeper. He had no business kissing her this way out in the open where any of his neighbors could observe, but at the moment he didn't care. The only thing he cared about was kissing Charlene, tasting her.

He ignored the warning bells, he disregarded the danger signs. All his body and mind could comprehend was both need and greed. Warmth was spreading all over him, shooting right to his

groin area. He wanted her. That fact he understood. And whether she knew it or not, she wanted
him too. He could tell in the way she was kissing
him back. All they needed was a bed…and, oh
yeah, a little privacy.

He quickly remembered again just where they
were and grudgingly pulled away from her
mouth. "Come on, let's go inside," he whispered
hot in her ear while taking her hand in his.

He could tell the instant she regained her
senses. She pulled her hand away from his.
"Why? No. We can't. We need to talk."

He couldn't help but smile at all the words that
tumbled out of her mouth. A mouth he wanted to
devour again. "Okay, let's go inside and talk.
Anything in particular you want to discuss?"

She looked at him as if he were dense. "You're
suggesting breaking and entering and you want
to know what in particular I want to discuss?
What about the thought of being arrested? How
does that sound for starters?"

He began walking and noted that she was moving beside him. "Not good. You're right. Forget
the idea."

"Now you're sounding reasonable," she said,
nodding.

"It's something I can do on my own. You stay here until I return."

She stopped walking and swung around and stared at him as if he'd completely lost it. "What! Are you crazy?"

"Don't think so," he said, smiling at the way she got overexcited at the least little thing. He wondered if she showed that same degree of excitement in the bedroom.

When they were back at his place he took the keys out of his pocket to open the door. He followed her inside, closed it behind them and leaned back against it. "Has anyone ever told you how cute you are when you get stirred up about something?"

She took off her jacket and tossed it across a chair before giving him an irritated look. She then crossed her arms over her chest. "This isn't funny, Drey."

His gaze moved from her face to her chest, more specifically, her breasts. The way her arms were folded lifted the twin globes up, pressing them against her blouse where he could clearly see the nipples. "No, it isn't funny," he said. "I might find a number of things amusing but never what I'm looking at now."

He could tell that at first she didn't comprehend what he'd said, but seconds after she did, she quickly dropped her hands by her sides at the same time he heard her grit her teeth.

He slowly crossed the room to pull her into his arms and kiss her. Surprisingly, she didn't resist him. Moments later he disconnected their mouths and then proceeded to cradle her face in his hands and kiss her again. He didn't know any other woman who in addition to having a high degree of sensuality was capable of igniting his enthusiasm for any little thing. Go figure.

Moments later, he withdrew his mouth from hers thinking he would never get tired of kissing her. The feel of her lips beneath his was a sensation he just couldn't explain. "I think I'll kiss you every time you get pissed off with me about something," he said softly. "Anger must do something to your taste buds. Electrify them. Make them addictive."

He then stepped back and gestured over to a huge book cabinet on one of the walls. "There's a bunch of movies in that top drawer over there if you want to watch one while I'm gone. And if you get bored doing that, you can tackle all those video games that I—"

"I'm going."

He frowned. "No, you're not."

"Yes, I am."

He shook his head. "What you said by the pond made sense. There's no need for the both of us to go to jail, so you stay here."

"I'm going, Drey. You don't know your way around once you get inside. Besides, you won't know what you should look for. You'll need me to identify just what you need."

He stared at her. She did have a point. "Okay, then, let's get moving. Like I said earlier, you need to change into dark clothes."

She nodded and then he watched as she rushed off toward the guest room.

They were both going to end up in jail, Charlene thought as she stood with her body pressed close to Drey's while he used something that looked like a hair clip to force their way inside. And this might not be the best time to think about it, but she thought he smelled super good.

"And you're sure there's not an alarm system?" he asked her over his shoulder.

"I'm sure."

It was dark but she didn't need any lights to see the dangerous yet sexy glint in his eyes. She had noticed them on the drive over. Whether he admitted it or not, she knew he was enjoying this. She could just see the headlines now.

Former Police Officer Arrested for Breaking into Coroner's Office.

She hadn't figured out yet just how they would broadcast her part in it, but there was no doubt in her mind that they would. At that point she would have to kiss her job goodbye. She should never have insisted on coming, but then she couldn't imagine watching a video while waiting for him to come back.

Charlene heard a click and knew Drey had gotten the door open.

"Right or left?" he asked her in a whispered tone.

"Left then straight for around 5 feet and then turn right," she responded. They would not be turning on any lights other than a penlight he held in his hand. They would stop by her desk to get the key that would open the file cabinet where the autopsy reports were kept. They intended to get both Harmon's and Joe Dennis's autopsy records. Then they had agreed to search Nate's office for the missing key.

"Okay, here's your desk."

Charlene nodded and within minutes she had the key to the autopsy room in her hand. "I got it," she whispered. And then she gave him directions on how to get to the autopsy room from where her desk was located.

Reaching their goal was done with little difficulty, but that didn't stop fear from flowing down Charlene's spine. Although the coroner's office didn't have an alarm system, it did have a security guard on payroll who made periodic checks. The key was to get in and out between the security officer's visits.

Drey whispered most of his words while she quickly opened the file cabinet and began thumbing through for the autopsy reports on Harmon and Dennis. The penlight had been replaced by a slim flashlight and within minutes they had retrieved the reports they wanted.

"Where to now?" she whispered close to Drey's ear, trying to ignore the stirrings in the pit of her stomach. How could she be thinking of wanting him at a time like this?

They carefully made their way from the autopsy room toward Nate's office. At one point they paused when they thought they heard a sound and discovered it was only the hum and click of the air-conditioning system.

Drey and Charlene began searching Nate's office in earnest, making sure to return anything they picked up to its proper place. After a few minutes of searching they still had not found the key. However, they did come across a copy of Joe Dennis's original autopsy report. It was in a folder with other documents labeled "To Be Destroyed."

After searching high and low with no success in finding the key, Drey whispered, "Evidently the key has now changed hands. Let's not waste any more time in here looking for it."

Charlene was about to agree when they heard footsteps coming down the hall. Drey killed the beam from the flashlight immediately and pulled Charlene with him into a small closet in Nate's office.

Charlene was standing behind Drey and clench-

ing his shirt when fear gripped her. What if someone had heard them moving around in Nate's office
and had called the police? What if they had guns?

"Relax," Drey whispered. "Your breathing has
changed. Take it easy."

That was easy for him to say, she thought as
she pressed her body even closer to his back.
Panic surged through her and had her clenching
his shirt even tighter. From a crack in the closet
door she could see it was one of the security men
making his rounds. She might have been imagining it, but Drey didn't appear in the least bit nervous. He stood there, cool and ready for action.
Silently she prayed that they didn't see any

The security guard—who had a gun strapped
to his waist—seemed to linger in Nate's office
longer than necessary. Glancing over Drey's
shoulder and gazing through the crack in the
closet door, Charlene saw why. The man had
taken a seat on the edge of the desk and was using
the computer, namely the Internet.

She and Drey watched as the man signed on
and went to a pornography Web site. Her view
wasn't as good as Drey's but she saw enough to
know the man was enjoying looking at the photos

of all the naked bodies that appeared on the screen. It was downright embarrassing, Charlene thought, and wished there was some hole she could crawl into.

After about half an hour, it seemed the man finally remembered he had a job to do, and reluctantly signed off the computer. Charlene had been afraid of getting caught the entire time. Fear had clogged her throat at some point, making breathing difficult.

Once they were sure the man had left to go to another part of the building, Drey came out of the closet and pulled her with him. After having stood in the same cramped position for so long, her legs felt stiff and her joints ached.

"Come on," Drey said taking her hand. "We got most of what we came for. Let's get the hell out of here."

Chapter 11

An hour later after taking a shower Drey took the time to remember everything that had happened that night at the coroner's office. It had been like a scene from a James Bond movie. The only difference was that he hadn't had in his possession any of that fancy technology. But he had been stuck in a very dangerous situation with a beautiful woman—a woman who was now probably asleep, dead to the world, after tonight's action.

He hadn't failed to notice that Charlene hadn't

said much of anything during the ride home. And once they had gotten here she had said goodnight and raced off to the guest room.

While preparing for his shower he had heard the one in the guest bath going. Visions of her standing naked under a spray of water had given him a boner and he'd ended up taking a cold shower before settling down and taking a warm one.

Thinking back on the evening, he realized getting into the coroner's office hadn't been a complete waste of time. He had gotten copies of Harmon's and Joe Dennis's autopsy records, as well as the discarded original autopsy record for Dennis. But they hadn't found the key. Chances were Nate had gotten rid of it by giving it to whomever he was in cahoots with.

Feeling the need of a cold beer, he left his bedroom and was rounding the corner when he heard a sound. He stopped, glanced over at the window and saw Charlene standing there and staring out.

Drey paused and looked at her thinking she was definitely a picture of beauty wearing a long velour white bathrobe. Even from across the room he picked up her just-showered scent that mingled with vanilla.

He couldn't help noticing that she was shaking. The heat was on in the town house so he wondered what was wrong with her. Then he knew. She was having a flashback to what had happened earlier that night. She was probably thinking about what could have happened had they gotten caught. More than likely she was reliving the fear, the excitement and the intensity of the situation they had found themselves in.

"Charlene?"

He said her name softly and she turned. The look he saw in her eyes made him swiftly cross the room and pull her into his arms. "Hey, it's okay. You're safe now. We're both safe."

Inwardly he called himself all kinds of fool for letting her talk him into taking her. As a police officer he had been in such dangerous situations before, but she had not. However, tonight he had exposed her to danger and because of it, she was going through this. An aftershock.

Drey continued to hold her with her face buried in his chest. He whispered over and over that she was okay while her shaking continued. What she needed was something to drink, preferably a glass of wine. But he didn't want to leave her alone for the time it took to fix her one. He just wanted to stand there and hold her.

A few moments later the shivers in her body began to ease. He tried not to think about just how soft she felt in his arms, how nice she smelled or how good her body felt pressed up to his. And most of all, he didn't want to remember just how delicious her mouth tasted.

But he did remember. And when she lifted her head to stare into his eyes, he no longer saw tension in them. He saw desire so thick it made his breath catch. Before he could react in any way, she stood on tiptoe and placed her mouth on his. And then she eased her tongue into his mouth.

He wasn't exactly sure what was driving her, but he knew what was driving him when he took control of the kiss. It was as if something inside him snapped and he wanted to gobble her up. And the way she was returning the kiss let him know that she wanted to be gobbled up. He thought the other kisses they'd shared had been intense, but they couldn't compare to the heat and passion they shared now. There was nothing simple about this kiss. It was the hottest kiss he'd ever endured and he felt his entire body ignite in flames.

He tangled his hands in her hair, trying to keep her mouth immobile while he plundered it in pleasure, and when she pressed even closer to him, molded her body intimately to his, he felt an explosion just waiting to happen. He knew just where he wanted to be when it did.

Inside her.

That thought made him pull back to end the kiss. She wasn't in the right frame of mind for him to have such thoughts, and he refused to take advantage of her. He would do the right thing even if it killed him, and right now it almost was. His entire body was on fire. More than anything he wanted to make love to her. But he wouldn't.

"Why did you stop, Drey?"

He heard her words, felt her confusion and knew he would be honest with her. "Because you aren't in your right mind now. You're thinking that you want something you really don't."

She shook her head, disagreeing with him. Instead of saying anything verbally, she leaned up on tiptoe and took his mouth again and he didn't deny her. What he did do was fight for control, though he found it hard to do. This time it was she who finally pulled back. "I know what I want,

Drey. I know what I need," she said in a whisper. "I need you. Now."

He gazed into her dark eyes, saw the desire there. That same desire stabbed him in the chest and he was tempted to pull her back into his arms to taste her some more. To gobble her up again.

He remembered what he'd said after their first kiss and the promise he'd made about not taking his desire for her any further until she gave the word. Although she had just done so, he wanted to make sure she understood what she was asking of him.

"You want us to make love?" he asked, so there wouldn't be any misunderstanding, no morning-after regrets.

"Yes."

He heard her response but pressed on to make absolutely certain. "I want to get inside you, Charlene. I want to make love to you the way a man makes love to the woman he wants, the woman he desires. I want to take you to the edge and back. I want to hear you scream, and in the end I want to make you come. Again and again. I want to feel it. Taste it. Are you absolutely sure those are the things that you want too?"

She stared at him, and he watched as she nervously licked her lips. She probably hadn't expected him to make things so blatantly clear. He watched her eyes darken and heard her breathy sigh before she said, "Yes, I'm sure that I want all those things. I want to share every single one of them with you."

In one smooth move Drey swept her off her feet and into his arms. He moved toward his bedroom, hoping she knew what she was agreeing to because he planned on keeping his word and making love to her all through the night.

Charlene's heart began beating faster the moment Drey placed her on his bed. A part of her wanted to tell him the truth about her experience level in the bedroom, but then another thought it best not to say anything. She needed him and she wanted him, and she wouldn't tell him that she was a virgin. He would find out soon enough.

Through heavy-lidded, desire-filled eyes, she watched as he stood back away from the bed to remove his clothes. This was the first time a man had ever undressed in front of her, and she was giving him her undivided attention. When he dropped his pajama bottoms, her breath caught.

His shaft was large, hard, thick and ready. She felt the muscles in her womanly core tighten, either in fear or anticipation.

Would she be able to handle that? Inwardly she forced herself to relax. She believed what he said. Under his skillful hands she would experience her first orgasm and she was looking forward to it. After everything she had gone through tonight, she needed it. She needed to be a part of him and wanted him to be a part of her. Regrets, if there were any, would come in the morning. But not tonight.

She then watched as he reached into a nightstand to pull out a condom packet. Several of them. The area between her thighs felt hot and edgy at the thought that he intended to make love to her more than once and hoped when he discovered that she was a virgin that he wouldn't change his mind.

He returned to the bed and reached out, and with practiced movement he removed her robe and nightgown. When she was completely naked before his eyes, he began touching her all over, letting his strong fingers cover her entire body, caressing it tenderly, methodically, while heightening the desire inside her.

He pressed her back in the bedcovers and stretched out beside her, allowing his mouth to discover the same areas his fingers had earlier. He tongued her throat, down her neck before moving lower to her breasts. She was aware of the throbbing of her pulse the moment he captured one hardened nipple between his teeth, lavishing it and torturing it all at the same time. And then she felt him ease his hand between her legs and she shivered at his touch. When he began to stroke it with the pad of his thumb, the sensations were so intense that her hips rose off the bed. It had to be the most erotic thing she had ever felt in her life.

She heard a moan and realized it came from deep within her throat, but Drey kept his mouth on her breast while his hand continued to fondle her between the legs.

"Drey."

His name came forth from her lips on a breathless sigh and she had no idea why she was calling it. She didn't want him to stop, but she wasn't sure she could handle the pleasure overtaking her, gripping her in a way she had never experienced before.

He raised his head up to whisper, "Relax,

Charlene, and let me take you on a pleasurable journey. There are parts of your body that are more sensitive than others. I plan on touching and tasting every one of them. There is a Chinese way of lovemaking that increases one's sexual pleasure while at the same time stimulating one's mind. I want to use several demonstrations of it tonight. Is that all right?"

"Yes." Somehow she had managed to get the single word past her lips while a ripple of fierce excitement passed through her. He began caressing her body again with his fingertips, and she could feel the heat gather beneath his hand. When it reached her thighs, she felt herself getting wet.

He shifted positions and his mouth took over for his hand. She released a small whimper the moment his tongue touched her there and she reached out, at first to pull his head away but then to hold it there while his mouth did some scandalous things to her womanly core, devouring it as if it was something he had to have. And then she felt a mirage of sensations overtake her, making her entire body appear to be coming apart and exploding in several pieces. She felt as if she were falling into a sea of pleasure that was destined to drown her.

"Drey!"

She screamed his name when an orgasm struck her, flinging her into mindless bliss and intense satisfaction. Shivers rammed through her and she heard herself moan over and over again. Moments later, when the last quake had subsided, Drey lifted his head, licked his lips and then leaned upward and kissed her, letting her taste the essence of her off his mouth.

He pulled back enough to put on a condom, and then he was covering her body with his. She met his gaze, wanting to warn him that this was the first time she had ever been intimate with a man, but afraid if she did so he wouldn't finish what he started. And she would die if he didn't. Her body felt too alive and sensitized for him not to carry this to completion.

She felt him ease her thighs apart just moments before the tip of his manhood touched the entry of her femininity. It felt huge, engorged and hot. It was as if it needed to be inside her to cool off. And then she felt him slowly easing inside her, stretching her and going so far and not being able to go any farther.

Their gazes held and she felt him place his

hands beneath her hips just before he leaned forward to kiss her again. Then suddenly, she cried out in his mouth the moment he pushed forward in a hard thrust, going inside her to the hilt. Pain came and went, yet he paused to give her body time to adjust to him and his size. It felt as if he was locked inside her, had completely taken over her lower body.

And then he began moving, slowly, in and out, demonstrating his power and skill with every thrust he made, while at the same time building pleasure within her yet again. Over and over he brought her to the brink of a mind-blowing orgasm, only to snatch it back and make the sensations ripple through her once more. She wondered why he was torturing her this way. She heard her own pleas for release from the tension he was steadily building inside her.

And then it seemed to peak and she screamed at the same time her body exploded, actually broke into a million fragmented pieces, melted into liquid. But he kept moving on top of her, thrusting rapidly, deeply, and on the heels of one orgasm she felt another. And then another. It was as if he was determined to see how many she could have.

Then she felt his body buck on top of her. Heard her name forced from his lips between gritted teeth. She felt him explode inside her. And then as if he had some sort of control over her body, she felt sensations flow between them that triggered more pleasure deep within her, and she felt herself drowning in ecstasy all over again.

He had warned her that he would make her come all night, but she hadn't accepted the truth of his words until now.

Chapter 12

The next morning Drey woke up to find a soft body wrapped around him. He remembered the events of last night and felt his heartbeat kick up a notch.

Charlene Anderson had not only turned out to be a surprising lover; she had been totally different from any woman he'd ever been with. She had been a virgin—something he was definitely curious about—yet she had managed to pull passion and desire out of him that he'd never felt before. And he had kept his promise. He had taken their lovemaking to the max and had made her come not only once, but all through the night. He couldn't remember the last time he had made love to a woman all night long.

She had to be totally exhausted. Chances were she would sleep most of the day. The only time they had taken a break was after that first time when he had discovered she was a virgin. He had taken her into the bathroom and placed her in a tub of warm, sudsy water and had joined her there and held her in his arms. Then after drying them both off, he had taken her back to bed and made love to her again, over and over.

Knowing if he didn't get up he would be tempted to make love to her again, he eased out of bed. As much as he enjoyed being with her, inside her, tasting her, he had work that needed to be done. And the first thing on his list was to go over those autopsy reports they had taken from the coroner's office last night. He would use the time she slept to do so while enjoying a cup of coffee.

But when she woke up…

He felt his body get hard just thinking of how their day might end up. They were lovers now and he couldn't see them going back to business associates or friends. He couldn't bear the thought of not making love to her again. There was so much he wanted to teach her, share with her. Last night proved she was a willing student, and as he had told her before, she was a very passionate woman. He knew the degree of that passion had astounded even her last night. She had wanted more and he had delivered each and every time.

After slipping back into his pajama bottoms he remembered he had a meeting with the Braddocks later today. He intended to tell them everything he knew about the case so far. Well, almost everything. He still wasn't ready to tell them that he knew the identity of Daiyu Longwei and more specifically, her relationship to Harmon Braddock as well as to him.

A half hour later he was in his office concentrating on the autopsy reports. A ripple of pain went through him while reading about the extent of Harmon's injuries, the man who was his biological father. That he had been murdered caused anger to mix with that pain.

He then compared the original autopsy report on Joe Dennis to the new one. Among numerous inconsistencies was one constant—neither report mentioned a key.

The only living relative Joe Dennis had was a nephew who lived in Dallas. Drey had contacted the man by phone and according to him, he and his uncle had not been close and there wasn't much the man could share with him about any friends Dennis might have had.

Typically if a death was ruled a homicide, the police would question neighbors who'd been home at the time. But since, thanks to Nate Ganders, Dennis's death would not be ruled a homicide, no one would be asking questions. At least no one but him. It was time for him to start sniffing around as of today. He would get access to Dennis's home and poke around and see what he could find.

"Drey?"

He didn't have to look up to know Charlene had entered the room. He felt her presence immediately, in every part of him, especially in his shaft. It hardened immediately.

She was standing in the doorway, wearing only his T-shirt which she had evidently taken out of his drawers. That she had gone through his stuff to find the T-shirt didn't bother him. In fact, the thought that she was wearing something of his over her naked skin sent a surge of excitement through him. Mainly because it was skin he knew the taste of, skin that he had rubbed against his own and touched all over.

He started to stand and decided not to. The last thing he wanted her to see was the size of his erection. No telling what she would think if she saw it. Besides, although she had willingly participated in last night's activities, today was the morning after and he wasn't sure what her attitude might be. For all he knew, she might have regrets about last night. So he would sit right there and follow her lead and hope it was positive. He wasn't sure how he would handle things if it wasn't. He couldn't tell from her expression how things would go. And that made him nervous.

"Charlene, you're awake," he said in a gravelly cautious tone.

"Yes, sorry about that. I should have awakened sooner," she said, still standing in the same spot. He tried to keep his eyes focused on her face and not allow them to travel down the length of her to see beyond where his T-shirt stopped midthigh. She had a nice pair of legs—long and smooth—

and he could distinctly recall how he'd felt being between them. The memory made his shaft grow another notch.

"No, you needed your rest," he heard himself say. He leaned back in his chair. Again he tried to keep his gaze on her face but found it straying downward. He cleared his throat when he felt his pulse rate increase. "What are your plans for today?" he asked.

She shrugged her beautiful shoulders. He knew for a fact that they were beautiful because he had seen them last night, bare. "Don't know. It depends on you," she said softly.

He smiled at her, although uncertainty was still eating away at him. "In what way?"

She stepped closer into the room, and he couldn't help it when his gaze lowered and feasted not only on her legs but her hips, thighs, ankles and feet. Seeing the parts of her that he had come into intimate contact with the night before sent a stirring of deep pleasure through him, aroused him even more. "In how do you feel the morning after?" she asked.

That was the same concern that he had for her. Did she hold the came uncertainty that he did?

Did she honestly think he would regret what they had shared the night before? "How do you think I should feel?" he decided to ask.

She took another step into the room and he watched her, getting more aroused by the second. "Not sure. I can only go by what I was told," she said.

Now he really was confused. "What exactly were you told and by whom?"

"His name was Carlos and he said that most men had a problem with overaged virgins."

He lifted a brow. "I thought we already covered the fact that I'm not like most men. Besides, you're no longer a virgin. But even if you would have confessed to being one before we made love last night, that would not have stopped me."

Her expression seemed unsure. "It wouldn't?"

"No."

"Why not?"

He couldn't believe she was asking him that, but from the look on her face, he could tell she really needed to know. "Mainly because I wanted to make love to you. Knowing beforehand that you were a virgin only meant I needed to handle you another way. I would have known to be gentler.

But make no mistake about it, Charlene. I would not have changed anything else. I would still have taken you as many times as I did and made love to you using those same various positions. Knowing you were inexperienced didn't dull the sensations of being inside you. Last night's sex was good between us and I have no doubt in my mind that it will only get better."

He stood. "Come here and let me show you what I mean."

She didn't hesitate in crossing the room to him but was surprised when he pulled her down in his lap facing him. She felt his body part beneath her, hard and throbbing beneath her naked bottom.

In one swift movement he pulled his T-shirt over her head, and before she could make a startled gasp, his mouth latched on to her breast. Each pull by his mouth triggered an arousal deep in her stomach. He was stirring up desires deep within her, primitive needs and wants.

And then he stood with her in his arms and, placing her on her feet, worked the pajama bottoms from his body, leaving them both totally naked. He lifted her onto his desk, widening her legs to stand between them and aiming his shaft straight for her feminine core. He eased her closer to it and when she felt it there at the entrance, she met his gaze.

Her heart began pounding as he began easing inside her, gripping her hips to hold her in place and accept his entry. She threw her head back when sensations began building inside of her and she closed her eyes.

"No. Open your eyes and look at me. Watch me bring you pleasure."

She did.

He wrapped her legs around his waist and locked her in. Over and over again he thrust inside her, making pleasure so intense overtake her.

Then suddenly he went still.

She met his gaze and saw shock in them when he said, "I forgot about a condom."

She fully understood what he was saying. "I'm on the pill to regulate my periods," she whispered. "Now, please…" Her body was in a feverish pitch and needed release.

He began moving again, and each thrust into her went deeper, faster, until she couldn't take any more. She screamed out his name as her body exploded and she felt his release, thick and hot, shoot inside her, at the same time.

One orgasm led to another and another and some time later she lay spent on top of his desk with his throbbing member still buried deep inside her. "I think we need to take this to the bedroom now," he whispered, lifting her body in a way that kept them connected.

She wrapped her arms around him thinking she had to be dreaming. Nothing could be this perfect, this sensual, this earth-shatteringly blissful. But she knew once they got to the bedroom, Drey would proceed to show her that it could.

"Let's get dressed. I have somewhere to go and I want you to go with me," Drey said, gently rubbing his hand along her thighs. He'd never been possessive when it came to a woman, not even the least tiny bit. But for some reason he was with her and unashamedly so.

"Where are we going?" she asked, leaning over to nibble his ear.

He knew if he didn't stop her she would take her newfound sexual confidence to a level of no return for them and she would find herself flat on her back beneath him yet again. They had made love most of the morning and then had showered together only to end up making love again after their shower.

He stood and placed her on her feet. "We're going to meet the Braddocks."

Chapter 13

Charlene knew all eyes were on her when she walked into Malcolm Braddock's office by Drey's side. She knew Malcolm by both name and face since he was currently embroiled in a heated campaign with a man by the name of Clint Hardy. Both were vying for the congressional seat left vacated as a result of Harmon Braddock's death. The special election was to be held at the end of the month and if the recent polls were reliable, Malcolm had a substantial lead.

Malcolm, the oldest at thirty-two, was tall,

with coffee-brown eyes and dark brown hair. Charlene thought he was a very handsome man and from what she'd read in the papers a few months ago, he was engaged to marry Congressman Braddock's former executive assistant, Gloria Kingsley. There would be a Christmas wedding at the family estate.

Although she did not know the others, Drey had filled her in as to who would be attending the meeting. Shondra Braddock, the late congressman's daughter, and Tyson Braddock, the late congressman's younger son.

Like Malcolm, Shondra was tall, with long dark hair and dark brown eyes. An attorney, she always had it together and from what Charlene had heard, she was not only beautiful, but highly intelligent. According to Drey, Shondra was so convinced her father's death hadn't been an accident that she followed up on a lead by going so far as to go work for the company where Harmon's last phone call was placed. She met the CEO's son, Connor Stewart, a former jet-setting bachelor. The two eventually fell in love and according to Houston's society's column, Shondra and Connor were Houston's hottest couple.

The middle child, Tyson resembled his siblings. On the drive over Drey had told her that Tyson and his wife had been on the verge of getting a divorce but were now back together and expecting their first child.

Drey quickly made introductions, explaining who she was and why she was there. Malcolm was the first to ask a question. "So, Ms. Anderson, you actually saw this key?"

Charlene nodded and said to the three, "Yes, and I'm Charlene, please. Drey and I were able to get a copy of my boss's first autopsy report indicating trauma to the body before he was able to destroy it."

"And you have no idea why he changed it?" It was Shondra who asked.

It was Drey who answered. "No, although I have my suspicions. I have a strong feeling that Nate Ganders is being blackmailed. Otherwise, why would he warn Charlene off and suggest to her that she take time away from the job? It's apparent he didn't want to get her involved and seems to be doing everything he can to keep her out of it. She's moved in with me for a while for protection."

Tyson leaned against the edge of his brother's desk. "So you're operating on the theory that whoever killed our father is paying a lot of money to keep it covered?"

"Yes, and until we find that person, keep in mind that a murderer is still on the loose and he's struck twice—with your father and Joe Dennis—and he will strike again to keep his identity hidden."

"So what do you suggest that we do?" Shondra asked, agitation very clear in her voice.

"Right now I have a few more people to talk to," Drey said, glancing down at his notepad. "I'm hitting a brick wall at the police station. I hate to say it but I think a few people down there are in on this too. I hope I'm wrong but I have a gut feeling about it. The one guy down at headquarters that I know I can trust—my former partner—is out of town but is scheduled to return this week. I'm hoping he'll be able to check out some things and shed some light on a few inconsistencies I've found."

"And what about that employee at Stewart Industries? The one Connor spoke with? Daiyu Longwei. She clammed up when Connor questioned her about Dad's last phone call to her. Have you spoken to her at all?" Tyson asked.

Drey shook his head. "I've spoken with her, but she didn't have any more to tell me either. I'll keep working on it, though."

Charlene didn't say anything as she racked her brain trying to recall where she'd heard the name before. Daiyu Longwei...

"So, what's next?" Malcolm was asking Drey.

"I plan to talk to the congressman's associates to see if they recall him acting strangely during his last days. There had to be a reason for his un-scheduled trip to D.C."

"I suggest you start with Senator Ray Cayman and Judge Bruce Hanlon. They've known Dad for years and are two of his closest friends," Tyson said.

Drey smiled. "I'll certainly do that."

After his meeting with the Braddocks, Drey dropped Charlene off at his place before proceed-ing to the apartment building where Joe Dennis had lived. He wanted to question the man's neigh-bors about the night Joe Dennis died.

He spoke first with the elderly couple who lived across the hall, Fred and Eleanor Billings. Mr. Billings was eager to let him in, assuming he was a detective from the police department. When Drey informed the couple he was an investigator, the Billingses were surprised that after several calls to the police station, no one had come out to ask them questions about what they had heard that night. Drey was surprised as well.

According to Mr. and Mrs. Billings they had been trying to watch their favorite television show and couldn't do so for all the loud noise coming from across the hall. Two men were yelling at each other at the top of their lungs. They had gotten so loud the Billingses had been tempted to call the police for disturbing the peace. In less than an hour the noise had stopped and the next day they had heard that Mr. Dennis—who they thought was a nice hardworking man—had died. Even though the recent news update indicated he had died of natural causes, the couple still questioned why no one wanted to hear what they had to say.

Drey visited several more of Joe Dennis's neighbors, but each one said they hadn't seen or heard a thing that night. One lady questioned why he was asking around when the papers said he'd died of natural causes. He had explained that he just wanted to collect all the facts.

It was getting late and he decided to put off contacting Senator Cayman and Judge Hanlon until tomorrow. What he wanted to do more than anything was to head home and mess around with Charlene some more. Memories of how they had spent their night and this morning caused his nerve endings to react. He loved her taste so much that he could bury his head between her legs and stay there. But then he also enjoyed being inside her, moving in and out and feeling her inner muscles clamp tight as they tried to squeeze everything out of him.

There were other things he enjoyed about her that weren't related to sex. He liked the way she went tit-for-tat with him, how she could make some offhanded comment in a way that made him smile. And he appreciated her sense of humor. His face broke into a lopsided grin when he thought of introducing her to his mother. Daiyu would like her.

His mother.

He then remembered how his mother's name had come up during their meeting with the Brad- docks. Sooner or later he would have to tell them the truth, but that would be only after he discovered for himself why Harmon had been trying to reach his mother that night. Had he suspected his life was about to end and wanted to leave her with some information? If that was the case, why Daiyu instead of his wife, Evelyn, or one of his kids? Why not his friends Senator Cayman or Judge Hanlon?

There were a lot of questions yet to be answered, but right now the only thing Drey wanted to think about was the sexy woman sharing his condo.

Charlene paced the room deep in thought. Now, where had she heard the name Daiyu Longwei from? It had first struck her as familiar when they had met with the Braddocks, and the nagging feeling wouldn't go away.

She had meant to ask Drey about it, but while Drey had been driving back from Malcolm Braddock's office her cell phone had rung. Her mother had been in a talkative mood. Nina had wanted to know how her relationship was progressing with the young man she had gone out of town with. Charlene felt her mother didn't need to know that things had progressed so well that she was no longer a virgin.

Thoughts of what she and Drey had shared since last night had her heart racing. She never knew a man could have so much energy when making love. Multiple orgasms were common for him, as well as being able to go for long periods of time without stopping. He'd seemed insatiable.

She'd been surprised at the extent of her own stamina. Granted, there had been pain at first, but after that, she had enjoyed his well-timed strokes into her body, the way he wouldn't hesitate to kiss her all over, as well as his knowledge of a woman's pleasure points. He had done everything last night that he'd said he would do. He had tasted her all over, had made her scream more times than she could count, had given her enough orgasms to last a lifetime and had remained inside her body for a long while…even when they had slept.

She had awakened that morning feeling totally rejuvenated and well rested, although she hadn't gotten much sleep. And then later, what they had done in his office, right there on his desk, made her blush. It was simply amazing how a woman could go from a virgin to a naughty sexual vixen overnight.

She was about to go into the kitchen to unwind

with a glass of wine when Drey's phone rang. She wondered if it was that woman Karen calling again and figured she would know soon enough if the woman left a message.

"Drey, mail came for you today. I think it's about your high school class reunion. You can drop by and pick it up anytime. Love you."

She smiled knowing the caller was Drey's mom and that he—

Charlene blinked when she suddenly thought of something. Walking quickly into Drey's office, she went straight to a photograph he had framed on the wall. It was a photo of him and his mother on the day he had graduated from the police academy. A gold plate beneath the picture said "Daiyu Longwei and Her Son, Drey St. John."

Confusion began snarling Charlene's thoughts. She studied the photographed again. She wasn't sure exactly how long ago the photo had been taken, but Drey's mother was definitely still an Asian beauty. It didn't look as if she'd aged that much at all from the photo Drey had hanging in his living room.

Another thought popped into her head when she recalled the meeting earlier at Malcolm

Braddock's office. She shook her head. Something didn't make sense.

She turned and walked out of Drey's office at the same time she heard the key turn in his door, alerting her that he had returned. The moment he closed the door behind him he glanced over at her and upon seeing her expression he quickly crossed the room and took her hand.

"What's wrong, Charlene?"

She stared at him, the man she had made love with all night. "I don't know, Drey. You tell me."

The brows covering his slanted eyes lifted and he released her hand. "And what do you want me to tell you?"

She held his gaze and asked, "Why didn't you tell the Braddocks that Daiyu Longwei is your mother?"

Chapter 14

Surprise held Drey immobile for one stunned moment and then he threw his car keys on the table. "I saw no need to do so." He then walked off.

Charlene followed and threw up her hands. "That doesn't make sense. You're handling a murder investigation for them and apparently your mother is somehow involved."

He swung around as a deep, angry frown covered his face. "You don't know that."

"Look, Drey, all I know is what I heard earlier. Your mother was the last person who talked to

Harmon. She apparently was the last person he tried to contact. Surely you want to know why."

"I've questioned my mother and she doesn't know why," he snapped. "And I don't want to discuss this investigation with you any longer."

She took a step and got in his face. "Fat chance! I had to leave my home because of this investigation. I'm not even sure I'll have a job to return to when all this is over, and you have the nerve to stand here and tell me you won't discuss it?"

He leaned in closer. A cold, hard look appeared on his face. "Yes, that's what I said. I don't want to discuss it."

And then he turned away and went into his office, closing the door behind him.

Drey leaned against the closed door and drew in a deep breath while his heart vibrated relentlessly against his ribs. No one was to know about his mother until he was prepared to tell it. He didn't want anyone asking those same questions that Charlene had just asked.

He gritted his teeth to keep from lashing out and hitting something. The last thing he wanted was to be on bad terms with Charlene, especially when she was right. He did owe her an explanation. Because of trying to help with his investigation she had been forced to leave her home and could possibly have lost her job.

But he wasn't ready to share with anyone how his world had gotten shattered a few weeks ago. He was still trying to work things out for himself. And he needed more time to do so. Problem was that time had run out. Charlene had figured out the truth and wanted answers. Answers she had a right to have. He could tell from the look on her face that he had hurt her feelings, something he hadn't intended to do. He was about to open the door and go talk to her when he heard his front door slam shut.

Damn!

He quickly came out of his office and crossed the room to snatch open his front door, only to see Charlene drive off in her car. Where in the hell was she going? And more importantly he wondered if she would be coming back. Thinking there was a possibility that she wouldn't come back made his gut clench. His chest suddenly felt tight.

He had never waited on a woman to come back to him before, but he would wait on Charlene Anderson.

Charlene had no idea where she was going. All she knew was that she needed distance from Drey. Going into separate rooms hadn't been far enough for her. She hadn't wanted to be under the same roof with the man.

Deciding the best thing to do was to walk off her anger, she headed in the direction of the mall, and then quickly changed her mind. The last place she needed to go was some place where she might be recognized. Instead she thought she would go to a movie at one of those theaters on the outskirts of town.

A part of her wished she could go to her own house and sleep in her own bed tonight. But, was that what she really wanted after having slept in Drey's bed? She knew the answer without much thinking. No. But she also knew she needed more from Drey than sex. She needed him to trust her enough to tell her what was going on. But why would he trust her? She was nothing to him but a temporary bed partner. Wasn't that what he'd once told her was all he needed? Men didn't have to confide in women they didn't intend to keep around. She refused to acknowledge the pain she felt in her heart. Nor could she acknowledge that she had fallen in love with him.

She thought about what he'd said and the degree of anger with which he'd said it. Her thoughts then shifted to last night and earlier that day, when he had made love to her with a gentleness that had almost brought tears to her eyes.

Yes, she loved him. It was her issue, her personal problem. But it would never, ever be her regret.

Drey stopped pacing long enough to glance down at his watch. It had been three hours and it was now dark outside. Where was she? He had tried reaching her on her cell phone a number of times but hadn't gotten an answer. Evidently she was too mad at him to return his call. He had even called her home number on the off chance she'd gone there, though he refused to think she would put herself in danger by doing that.

After he had time to fully think about it, he had called himself all kinds of fool for saying what he had to her. She definitely deserved an apology and an explanation—if she would only return to listen.

His breath caught when he heard a car door slam and automatically he moved to the door. If it was Charlene, she would knock since he hadn't yet given her a key. His heart began racing when he heard footsteps moving up his walkway and he knew it was Charlene. It just had to be.

Too eager to wait for her knock, he opened the door and there she stood, utterly beautiful in the moonlight with a startled look on her face. "Sorry," he said softly. "I didn't mean to scare you."

She shrugged. "No harm done."

His gaze caressed her face before he stepped aside, allowing her entrance. Hoping she was there to stay and hadn't just come to pick up her things. "If you're hungry we can order out," he said.

She walked into the foyer and turned around after placing her shoulder bag on the table. "Thanks, but I'm not hungry. I took in a movie and grabbed a couple of hot dogs while I was there."

"Oh." So that's where she had gone. "Well, if you've got some time I'd appreciate it if we talked."

She placed her hands in her back pocket and tilted her head back to meet his gaze. "What about?"

"What I didn't want to talk about earlier."

Her gaze lowered to the floor. "You don't have to do that."

"Yes, I do." And he honestly knew that he did. He could feel the strain between them, the distance. He didn't want that. He wanted things the way they were last night. He wanted the closeness.

"All right, then. Talk."

"Can we sit down in the living room?"

She shrugged again. "Sure. Why not?"

He watched as she went to sit on the sofa, folding her legs beneath her. With his heart still racing nonstop, he took the chair across from her, when what he really wanted to do was reach out and pull her into his lap and kiss her. But he knew he couldn't do that. He had screwed up and had to backpedal. Get back into her good graces. Literally, he had to do something he had never done with a woman before—bare his soul.

He was a private person. No other woman had ever reached beyond that area of "do not enter" with him. But Charlene had invaded his space. In just a short period of time she had gotten totally and completely under his skin. And last night he had gotten under hers in the most intimate way. He had been inside her, places where no other man had ever gone. He had branded her with his markings all over her body and didn't regret doing so. And if given the opportunity he wouldn't hesitate to do it again.

"First, I want to apologize for lashing out at you earlier, Charlene. I had no right to do that. You deserve to know what's going on with the investigation, every aspect of it."

He paused a moment before continuing. "What I'm about to tell you is something I haven't told anyone yet, especially the Braddocks. But I will eventually tell them because they too have a right to know. I took this case before knowing it myself. While I was investigating, my mother's name come up as the last person the congressman spoke with. My mother says she honestly doesn't know why he called her and I believe her. But something I do know is that the two of them had a history."

"What sort of history?" she asked quietly.

He was silent for a moment and then he said, "My mother and Congressman Braddock had an affair many years ago, before I was born and before she married my father. She was young, inexperienced and thought she was in love, and yes, he was a married man at the time. However, it's my understanding that he and his wife, Evelyn, were going through some things. That does not excuse his behavior or my mother's."

Charlene nodded and then said, "I can see your reluctance to spring that on the Braddocks."

"Yes, but there's more. It goes a lot deeper than that."

She leaned forward in her seat. "Deeper in what way?"

He swallowed and felt a sudden tightness in his chest. This was the first time he would admit this to anyone. He spoke, hearing the words as he said them. "Congressman Braddock was my biological father."

Chapter 15

A stunned expression covered Charlene's face. "Your father!"

"Yes, my father. However, I didn't find out until I questioned my mother as to why the congressman would call her and just how they knew each other."

Charlene stared at him and immediately she knew that admitting such a thing had been hard for him. "And Ronald St. John? He was your—"

"He is the only father I know. I can't deny it was Harmon Braddock's seed that made me, but it was Ronald St. John's love that shaped me into who I am today. He's the person I remember from the time I was in the crib, who had always been there for me. The person who took me to my Little League games, showed up at every activity I was in while attending school and the person who made me believe I could do anything. Ronald St. John is the man I consider my father."

Charlene eased to the edge of her seat. She could tell Drey still had a hard time accepting that biologically, he was a Braddock. "Didn't you say that the congressman was your mentor?"

"Yes."

"To me that means he wanted to share some aspect of your life."

Drey nodded. "My mother said basically the same thing."

"Don't you believe her?"

He leaned back in his chair. "It's not that I don't believe her, Charlene. I just don't care. Braddock had his family and Ronald St. John had his. I consider myself a St. John."

"But truly you are a Braddock." There, she'd said what he evidently needed to hear. He couldn't deny who he was, not when Braddock blood ran through his veins.

He stood and walked over to the window and glanced out. She knew he was thinking. Moments later he turned to her. "I don't know how I'm going to tell them, but I know I have to. I'm even doubtful that their mother knows about me. It's my understanding that she's aware that Harmon had an affair and with whom, but she doesn't know that a child had been conceived out of it. I don't want to do anything to tarnish her husband's memory."

Charlene didn't know what to say because that was a good possibility when Mrs. Braddock discovered the truth.

He interrupted her thoughts by saying, "And then the siblings might be resentful."

She wondered if he was afraid that would happen. Was he concerned that his siblings would reject him because of what their father and his mother had done thirty-three years ago? "I don't know, Drey. I met them today and they seem a pretty confident yet wholesome trio."

"They are close."

"Yes, I can tell they are," she said slowly. "But that doesn't mean they won't let you in or that—"

"I might not want to get in."

He did, Charlene immediately thought. Otherwise he wouldn't be carrying so much on his shoulders. What would it take to make him see that no one could blame him for the congressman's and his mother's actions all those years ago?

Suddenly, something hit her. *Drey needed her.* She wasn't sure just where that thought or idea came from; it was just there, in her mind and in her heart. It was still strange how quickly things had progressed between them, but they had. And although he might never admit to any feelings for her, she knew at that moment she had to have meant something to him for him to have shared that with her. Okay, she wasn't about to operate under any false illusions. In all honesty, she knew exactly where she stood with him. But for her, it didn't matter. She loved him and would always love him and would be there for him until he said it was time for her to go. She would love to share more with him, but he had a wall erected, one she doubted she could scale.

She slowly walked over to where he was standing. For a long moment she stood silently beside him and looked out at the same pond, saw the same ducks and for a little while felt the same sense of peace.

"So now you know," he finally said softly, without looking over at her.

"Yes, now I know. Thanks for sharing." She then stood on tiptoe and kissed him on the cheek.

Automatically, he reached out his hand and captured her around the waist and pulled her closer to him. She felt him, every hard part of him, while she gazed deep into his eyes. He was tall, well muscled and unmistakably male. And she was willing to accept that he would not love her back no matter how much she loved him. But that was okay. She could handle it. Didn't someone say it was better to have loved and lost than not to have loved at all?

"Are you still upset with me?" he asked, and the deep timbre of his voice felt like silk sliding across her skin.

"Not anymore. But promise me the next time that we'll talk through things," she said firmly.

"I promise."

The air between them suddenly felt hot, charged. Sexual tension was building, spreading. She could feel it the longer he looked into her eyes. Desire was vibrating in her veins, causing a ripple effect in her stomach. She watched his gaze shift slowly from her eyes to her mouth, and automatically she licked her lips.

"Let me do that for you," he said in a throaty voice and proceeded to lick her mouth from corner to corner. As she released a breathless sigh, he slid his tongue inside.

Caught, she thought, as she grabbed hold of it with her own and began mating with it, the way he had taught her to do last night. She felt him pull her deeper into his arms as she feasted on his mouth. When she had returned from the movies she had been wound up so tight, and now she was beginning to unravel, right in his arms, under the onslaught of his tongue.

He suddenly pulled back and shut the blinds. He then proceeded to tear his clothes off right there. She followed his lead. He finished undressing before she did and helped her get out of her clothes. The last piece to go was her panties and when he dropped to his knees to help her remove them she had a feeling where such helpfulness would lead.

He backed her up against the closed door for support, spread her legs and then buried his head between them. She heard his manly growl just seconds before his tongue invaded her, going deep and devouring her. She was no longer shocked by how much he enjoyed tasting her this way. She held her breath, fought back an intense scream as sensations tore into her, ripped through every part of her body, fizzled through her veins and electrified her pores.

And then he took his hands and lifted her hips, wrapped her legs over his shoulders so he could feast more. She was a goner. She felt the buildup inside her ready to burst and couldn't hold back any longer.

She screamed as an orgasm of gigantic proportions slashed into her. But that didn't deter Drey from his goal, which was to make her come again.

She did. But instead of screaming she released a deep, gutted moan while he continued to hungrily lap her up. And when she thought there was no way she could take any more, he quickly eased her legs off his shoulders and placed them around her waist just seconds before thrusting hard into her feminine core. He began pumping into her with whiplike speed, making her aware of every throbbing inch of him that was sliding in and out of her, stroking her insides with a skill and perfection that she found astounding.

The warmth of his breath stirred her ear as he whispered just what he was doing to her and how he was doing it. She wrapped her arms around his neck when she felt another orgasm coming on. And when he called out her name, she felt him explode deep inside her, shooting his hot release everywhere. She followed, tumbling into a sea of ecstasy that nearly drowned her.

Moments later, without disconnecting their bodies, he supported her back with the palm of his hand and with her legs still securely wrapped around his waist, he moved away from the door and carried her to his bedroom.

Drey stared at Charlene while she slept.

It was a crazy thing to do but a rather simple one, mainly because he liked looking at her, especially after they'd made love. He liked seeing the perspiration on her skin as well as the passion marks he'd put in various places. He liked seeing the peaceful look on her face and how her lips twitched on occasion while she slept.

To be quite honest, he liked everything about

her. Especially the way she gave herself to him, so unselfishly and with a thrill that excited him and heightened his desire for her.

When she shifted in sleep, he tilted his head to the side and gazed at her breasts. The tips of her nipples still looked hard, as if they begged to be licked. Or better yet, sucked. He could imagine her baby doing that very thing.

No, he couldn't imagine it because the baby would belong to some other man rather than him, and the thought that someone else's child would grow in her stomach was unacceptable.

Easing closer to her, he placed a hand on her waist. He wasn't used to feeling possessive, but around her you could call him Caveman Drey and it wouldn't bother him any.

Why?

Why was he so affected by her in a way he had never been by any other woman? The sex was good. Off the chain. But good, off-the-chain sex had never made him feel this way toward a woman. Ever. But then he had to admit making love to Charlene wasn't just good or off-the-chain. It was thrilling, sensational, mind-blowing. It was the kind that made you want to make love all night, all day, every chance you got. It was addictive.

But most importantly, it was theirs.

And he knew he would only feel this way with her, which suddenly made sweat bead on his forehead. He was getting hooked on her and for him that wasn't a good thing. He wasn't a man prone to having just one woman in his life. He didn't intend to settle down, now or ever. He liked having bed partners, not long-term girlfriends or, heaven forbid, a wife. It just wasn't in his makeup.

He would enjoy what they shared for now and then work her out of his system. When she left that would be it. He would bury himself in another case. And he would be fine. He would get over her. He had to.

Charlene woke with the sun shining in through the window. Her head lay nestled in the crook of Drey's shoulder and he was turned slightly toward her with one leg thrown over her thigh and one hand resting between her legs, tangled in the curls covering her femininity.

She glanced up and found him asleep, which was fine. It gave her time to think about last night.

He had shared himself with her, and later she had shared herself with him. She had no regrets. All she had was a happy mind and a satisfied body. She couldn't help but smile at that.

"Aren't we just full of cheer this morning?"

She glanced up and looked into Drey's smiling face. He was awake. "Yes, we are," she said, and then almost groaned out loud when his hand between her legs began moving.

"Like how that feels?" he asked in a husky voice. "Do you like for me to touch you this way?"

"Yes, I like it."

"Umm, I like it too. I like it especially when you get wet, like you're doing now. You're getting real wet. You know what that means, don't you?"

"Yes."

"Then ease over here. I want you to ride me this morning."

She slid her body over his, found him hard and ready and looked down into his face. "Is this all you want me to do?"

"For starters."

And then he lifted her up and eased her down on his shaft, connecting their bodies immediately when he slid into her. She began riding him and from the expressions that crossed his face, he was enjoying it. And so was she. She could get used to starting each of her mornings this way, but she knew that was only a dream. For now, though, she could make her dream a reality.

Drey glanced over at Charlene across the breakfast table. He had a busy day ahead of him. First he planned on meeting with Senator Cayman and Judge Hanlon, before paying a visit to Stewart Industries. There had to be a reason Harmon had been contacting his mother. Was there some specific information he had wanted her to find out for him but had gotten killed before given the chance to reveal it to her? Connor Stewart, who was currently dating Shondra, had welcomed his visit. Connor's father was CEO, but it was rumored the old man was about to step down and would name Connor as his successor.

"More coffee?"

He glanced across the table at Charlene and smiled. "No, but I'd love having more of you."

She chuckled. "You've had enough, thank you. Don't be so greedy."

"Ah," he said with an amusing glint in his eyes,

"you of all people have the nerve to call me greedy. You, who have become the multiorgasm queen."

Her smile unashamedly widened. "Yes. You know what they say. Practice makes perfect."

He laughed, not believing the conversation they were having at the breakfast table. "I want you to hold on to that thought until I return later."

"I will." Her expression turned serious then and she asked, "Do you think Congressman Braddock took either Senator Cayman or Judge Hanlon into his confidence and told them anything?"

"Not sure but I won't know until I ask. Once I tell them about my theory regarding the congressman's death not being an accident, I'm sure they'll want to help any way they can."

"I feel certain they will too."

Drey reached across the table and took Charlene's hand in his. "Miss me today."

She smiled and lifted the hand that held hers and kissed the back of it. "I will."

Chapter 16

The look on Judge Hanlon's face was one of shock. "What do you mean you think Harmon's death wasn't an accident?"

Drey knew it was a lot for the judge to believe but he answered anyway. "There are a lot of inconsistencies in the reports. And then there's Joe Dennis's death."

"But I thought Dennis died of a heart attack."

"It seems a lot of people think that as well."

The judge raised his bushy brows. "But you have reason to believe otherwise?"

"Yes, I have reason to believe otherwise." Drey decided not to go into details about the inconsistencies in the autopsy report. To do so meant revealing how they obtained the report. There was no way he could overlook the fact that Hanlon was a judge, one known as "Hard-time Hanlon." No criminal brought before him got off easily.

"Well, I hope you find the person responsible. Harmon and I go back a long way, all the way back to when the two of us were young upstart attorneys working in the prosecutor's office. That was over twenty years ago and we remained good friends since."

Drey nodded. "I won't rest until I find the person responsible."

"Good, now what can I do to help?"

"I just need to know if the congressman ever mentioned anything to you about Stewart Industries."

The judge rubbed his jaw in deep thought. "Not that I can recall. Why?"

"Because it seems the last call Harmon made was to there."

The judge looked surprised. "Why on earth would Harmon call there?"

Drey stood. "We don't know but that's just one of the many things I plan to find out."

The judge then stood as well. "Well, young man, if you find the person responsible, I want to try him or her in my court. If they're found guilty I promise they will pay for what they did to my friend."

Drey found Senator Cayman on the golf course and had to ride in the golf cart with him to hold a conversation. Now retired, the senator told of his and Harmon's friendship.

"You know," the older man was saying, "in a way I feel responsible for Harmon's political career. After about twenty years as a prosecutor, Harmon accepted a position as my head legal counsel and he was a darn good one. Worked for me for a number of years before deciding to run for political office himself. He was a darn good congressman. But…"

Drey lifted a brow. "But?"

"But even I would have to admit that the bill Harmon voted down a few years ago—one that would have helped a lot of needy families—surprised as well as disappointed a lot of people, especially Malcolm. That's when he walked away from the family."

Drey wondered why the senator was telling him that. Evidently his confusion showed on his face because the senator then added, "There's always a dirty side of politics, son."

Drey thought on his words before asking carefully, "And you think Congressman Braddock wasn't an honest politician?"

"I'm not saying that. The Harmon Braddock I knew was a very honest and upright man. But people can change. He wasn't perfect."

The senator's statement made Drey press on with his questions. "You and Harmon spent a lot of time together, right?"

"Yes. We played golf together at least once a week when he wasn't in Washington."

"Did he ever mention Stewart Industries to you?"

The older man thought on his question and then shook his head. "No, not that I recall. Why?"

The golf cart came to a stop and they got off near a beautiful pond. "We have reason to believe that he made his last telephone call to a person there."

The senator seemed to ponder Drey's words and then said, "Hmm, I find that interesting."

Drey lifted a brow. "And why is that?"

"Because Stewart has been in the news a lot lately. Everyone is wondering when the old man will be stepping down, and more importantly, if he'll make his son CEO when he does. I've often heard that fathers and sons have a difference of opinion when it comes to running a company. Personally, I think Connor Stewart would do a better job. He's smart, intelligent and a natural leader." The senator then gave a low chuckle. "And I understand he's something of a ladies' man."

Drey didn't comment. From what he could see, Connor Stewart's days as a ladies' man were over, since according to the gossip column of the local newspaper, there was speculation as to whether he and Shondra were secretly planning a June wedding.

"I appreciate you taking time to meet with me today, Senator."

"No problem." The senator then eyed him curiously. "How good are you with a club?" the older man asked.

Drey couldn't help but chuckle. "Fair."

"Well, if you ever want to get in any practice time, this is the place to be."

Drey smiled. "Thanks, I'll remember that."

The last person Drey needed to visit was Connor Stewart. A Matthew McConaughey look-alike with blue eyes and long blond hair, Connor worked hard and was all-business. On the other hand, Drey also heard Connor had a wild streak, which was the reason his father hadn't stepped down to make him CEO.

And just as Senator Cayman had said, Connor was something of a ladies' man...or he used to be. It had grown increasingly obvious to the media over the past couple of months that he was strictly wining and dining one woman—Shondra Braddock. Their interracial love affair was getting a lot of attention.

Drey had met Connor before and thought he was a likeable guy. "Thanks for seeing me," he said, taking the seat Connor offered.

"No problem. I know Shondra's mind will be eased when she finds out what really happened to her father and why."

Drey began asking him a series of questions,

trying to determine if there was any record of Harmon having any contact with Stewart.

Connor shook his head. "Trust me, if there was, Shondra would have discovered it long ago." He chuckled. "I'm sure you're aware that was her primary reason for taking a job here a few months ago. She was determined to undercover some wrongdoings with the company. She didn't find anything. However, we were able to trace Harmon's calls back to one of my employees, a competent woman by the name of Daiyu Longwei. I understand you've already spoken to her yourself."

Drey shifted uneasily in his chair. "Yes, I have."

"And I'm sure she's told you she doesn't know why the congressman was trying to contact her."

Drey spent the next few minutes going over some of the committees that the congressman was a part of to see if any were connected to Stewart Industries in any way. They didn't discover any.

When Drey stood to leave, Connor said, "I understand that you have a houseguest."

At Drey's raised brow, Connor smiled. "Shondra

mentioned it. She likes Charlene and appreciates the information she was able to pass on to you about the autopsy reports."

Drey nodded. "Yes, Charlene finding out about the false autopsy report made it obvious there was some sort of cover-up going on."

"Well, Shondra and I want to show our gratitude by giving you this," Connor said, offering a key to Drey.

At Drey's bemused look, Connor said, "It's the key to my beach house in Malibu. It's free for you to use this weekend. One of my pilots will be at your disposal to fly you there."

Drey reached out and took the key with a huge grin on his face. "Thanks. I'd love to take you up on your offer."

Drey let himself in the house later that day and immediately heard the sound of the vacuum cleaner. Finding Charlene in the hallway, he walked up to her and lightly tapped her on the shoulder. He hadn't wanted to scare her but could tell when she nearly jumped out of her skin that he had done so anyway.

"Why are you vacuuming?" he asked, pulling a

Houston Texans cap off her head to see how her hair tumbled to her shoulders. "I have a housekeeper."

She smiled up at him. "I know but I wanted to stay busy. I'm not a television person."

He pulled her into his arms thinking it had to be hard for her to spend her days with nothing to do. They had both agreed that the less she went out, the better. "Well, I have a surprise for you."

Her eyes lit up. "What?"

"As you know I met with Connor Stewart today, and he was gracious enough to offer me the use of his beach house in California for the weekend."

She eyed him skeptically before asking, "I know how busy you are with the investigation. Will you have time to get away?"

He smiled. "I'll make time as long as you come with me, and as long as we're back by Monday. I have another meeting with the Braddocks then." She clapped her hands, and her excitement, he thought, was infectious.

"Okay, I can guarantee those two things," she said happily.

He chuckled as he wrapped his arms around her. "Then let's start packing."

Chapter 17

Monday morning Drey eased out of bed and glanced over his shoulder at Charlene, who was sound asleep. They had returned to Houston late last night after having spent a wonderful weekend in Malibu. It had been a lazy weekend where they talked, made love, ate, made love and then repeated the process all over again.

He would be the first to say it was a weekend they both needed. During their talks they found out a lot about each other, and their walks on the beach had been extra, extra special. He stepped into the shower thinking of the meeting he was scheduled to have that day with the Braddocks. He really hadn't discovered anything new since their last meeting. The only good thing he would report was that his former partner with the police department had returned from vacation and was to report in today. He had left a message on his cell phone asking that they meet later today for a private conversation. If any of the cops on the force were dirty, he knew without a doubt that his former partner, Lavender Sessions, was clean.

Drey turned the water on full blast. He would surprise Charlene and prepare her breakfast in bed. She deserved it. He wasn't aware of just how vigorous a sexual appetite he had until he'd met her. The more he made love to her, the more he wanted her. All it took was a look, a touch and he was ready. She brought that out in him, a need he couldn't deny even if he tried. Because of her, he looked forward to his days and especially his nights. What he didn't look forward to was the day she would pack to leave, once he had solved the case and brought Harmon's and Dennis's killer to justice.

* * *

Charlene had gotten up to use the bathroom and through the shower glass door saw Drey amidst the steam. She could only stare at the body that had given her so much pleasure over the past week.

Every time she saw his nakedness, a buzz of desire would run through her. And whenever he looked at her through his slanted eyes, it was always in a way that no man had looked at her before. It was as if she were the only woman on this earth. The only woman he wanted.

She suddenly felt a throbbing sensation between her legs and could not understand, especially after their weekend and last night, how she could want him again so soon and with such intensity. She inhaled deeply, deciding not to try and understand it, just accept it as the way things were with them. They were two highly stimulated sexual beings who enjoyed making love to each other.

She shimmied the robe off her shoulders and began walking naked toward the shower. He hadn't seen her yet, but she knew pretty soon he would. He seemed to have a radar system that homed in on her no matter where she was. And she had no complaints.

Drey rubbed a wet hand down his face the moment he heard the shower door open. He reached out and pulled Charlene to him.

"Couldn't sleep?" he asked her in a deep, sexy voice.

She shook her head. "I woke up and you were gone. I missed having you inside me."

It had become the norm when they made love for the final time at night, he would pull her close and go to sleep still inside her. He had the uncanny ability to keep his erection hard while in her. For some reason he needed the connection of their bodies intimately entwined that way and it seemed that she did as well.

He reached out and pushed her hair away from her face to keep most of it from getting wet. "Do you know how beautiful you are?" he asked huskily.

"No," she said, smiling. "Are you going to tell me?"

"Yes. You're beautiful here," he said, lightly touching her lips. "And here," he said, tracing a hand down her chin and neck to fondle her breasts tenderly.

Charlene inhaled sharply from his touch. There was perfection in his fingers, she thought as her eyes gazed deeply into his. And then he leaned down and captured her mouth with his.

The moment their lips touched and their tongues tangled, she released a deep moan as a mirage of stimulating sensations invaded her. He took his time kissing her, as he usually did, stroking his tongue over hers while his hands continued to fondle her breasts, skimming over the hardened tips and making her moan even more.

And then she felt his hand move between her legs and he began touching her there, stirring sensations that begged for release.

She felt herself being lifted and knew the exact moment he had pressed her back against the shower wall, all without breaking their kiss. And when he wrapped her legs around his waist and then used his knee to spread those same legs apart, she knew what was coming.

She moaned deep into his mouth the moment he entered her, his engorged shaft invading her the very way she wanted, and the way she needed. When he began thrusting in and out of her with rapid precision, her moans became whimpers. Moments later, she quickly pulled her mouth away from his when she couldn't take any more.

"Drey!"

Screaming his name seemed to reach something primitive inside Drey. He threw his head back at the same time he thrust deeper inside her, hitting the very spot inside her he wanted to activate—her erogenous zone—and making her scream again. She screamed a third time when she felt the essence of his hot release flooding her, and then he was kissing her again with a hunger that always astounded her.

And that always made her love him even more.

She owed Drey a shirt, Charlene thought as she walked into the store at the mall. After their shower he had gotten dressed for his meeting with the Braddocks and she had gone back to bed. When he was ready to leave and had come into the room to kiss her goodbye, in a playful moment she had tried pulling him down in bed with her, only to rip a few buttons off his shirt. They had ended up making love again before he had gone into his closet to find another shirt to put on. He had teased her about owing him a shirt and she wanted to surprise him with it when he came home later.

She knew what store she wanted to make the purchase from and figured she would be in and out in no time. She felt wonderfully giddy at the thought of buying an item of clothing for him. Other than her father, she had never purchased clothes for a man before.

Charlene had selected a shirt she thought he would like and with the shirt in her hand, she was proceeding toward the cashier station when she heard a loud voice. Some man was arguing with a store clerk. She stopped dead in her tracks, her heart racing and the hairs on the back of her neck standing up. She recognized that voice. It was the same one that had argued with Nate that day in his office. The day before the autopsy report had gotten changed.

She looked around to see where the voice was coming from and whom it belonged to. She spotted him and recognized him immediately as a politician whose picture she'd seen numerous times in the newspapers.

Something made her move in that direction and she got close enough to see he was still giving the store clerk a hard time about a purchase he was trying to exchange. His voice continued to get louder.

She glanced down at his hand. He was holding his key ring, probably the one to his car. But what caught her attention was one of the keys on the ring. It was *that* key. The same one that had been on the autopsy table next to Joe Dennis's body. No wonder neither she nor Drey had been able to find it that night they had gotten into the coroner's office.

Realizing the smart thing to do was to leave before he got a chance to see her, she started to back up. At the same moment the man looked up and caught her staring. Her breath got logged in her throat, but she tried to appear normal. How could he possibly know who she was since their paths had never crossed? However, deciding she would not give him the chance to react one way or the other, she placed the shirt back on the stack and quickly walked out of the store. By the time she got to the parking lot she had begun running to her car.

She needed to contact Drey immediately.

Drey and his former partner, Lavender Sessions, who was now a detective with the Houston Police Department, met in private at Lavender's home.

"You know if I find out anything I'll let you know, Drey. And just so you'll know, I wasn't on vacation for the past couple of weeks like everyone assumes. I was in D.C.," Lavender was saying. "There is reason to believe some of the guys are on the take and the entire police corruption is centered on one man. We're working with the FBI to exposed his identity. It has spread into more areas than the police department and we want to stop it before it spreads any further."

Drey nodded. He then studied his friend, concerned for his safety. "Are you sure that you're safe and they don't suspect you of anything?"

Lavender smiled. "It's too soon for them to suspect anything. Just before I left for two weeks, I was approached to consider making extra money on the side. I knew then I was being asked to be a part of the bad guys. I'm supposed to give them my answer this week. I'll be the mole the FBI needs to bring things to an end."

Lavender continued. "And you're probably correct in thinking Congressman Braddock was murdered. He had contacted the FBI indicating he had some items to turn over. He never made it back to Washington."

Before Drey could respond, his cell phone rang. "Excuse me." He pulled it out of his jacket pocket and quickly flipped it open once he saw it was Charlene. "Yes, sweetheart?"

"I saw him, Drey," she said in a panicked tone. "I saw the man who was arguing with Nate that day. I recognized his voice. And he has the key. I saw the key that was taken out of Joe Dennis's stomach on his key ring."

Drey was out of his seat immediately. "Where are you?"

"The mall."

"The mall! But I thought we agreed that—"

"I know. I know," she said, cutting him off. "You can spank me later."

Any other time he would have found her statement amusing, but not now. Drey glanced over at

Lavender. He knew his friend had been following most of the conversation. Drey turned on the speaker to his cell phone and then placed it on the table between them. He wanted Lavender to hear everything. "Listen, Charlene. Can you tell if you're being followed?"

She paused and he figured she was looking out of her rearview mirror. "No. I ran out of the store and left immediately. I doubt he had time to follow me."

Drey nodded, relieved. "And you recognized the man?"

"Yes, Drey, you won't believe who he is."

Drey glanced over at Lavender. "Okay, who is he?"

Charlene let out a disgusted sigh before saying, "Judge Bruce Hanlon."

Drey instructed Charlene to meet him at home. When she got there he had arrived already with another man. He introduced her to Lavender.

"I need to alert the Braddocks," Drey said. "They consider Hanlon a family friend." Anger ripped through him when he remembered meeting with the judge last week. The man had pretended to be so concerned about how the investigation was going. Now Drey knew why.

"I've already contacted Washington," Lavender added. "They've notified FBI headquarters here. It appears things are going down sooner than we expected. It all makes sense now. The judge is the ringleader who's been working with a local crime family and taking kickbacks. Warrants are being prepared for everyone involved as we speak."

"Good," Drey said, pulling Charlene into his arms, not caring that Lavender was watching. He needed to hold her to make sure she was fine.

After a few moments she pulled back. "We need to go tell the Braddocks," she said. "Weren't you supposed to meet with them today?"

Drey nodded. "I did, earlier. They mentioned they would all be together at the family home this evening. They were joining their mother for dinner." He glanced at his watch. "Come on. They should be arriving now."

Drey and Charlene arrived in record time and were led by the housekeeper to the family room where the Braddocks and their significant others were sitting around talking. Everyone looked up, surprised to see them.

"Sorry to interrupt," Drey said, "but there has been a major development that I think all of you need to be made aware of immediately."

"What?" Malcolm said, coming to his feet, as the others gave Drey their undivided attention.

Drey glanced around. "Where's Evelyn?" he asked.

"She's taking a stroll in the flower garden," Shondra said. "Drey, what is it? What have you found out?"

Drey sighed, thinking maybe it was for the best that Evelyn wasn't present for this part. He knew how much she thought of Judge Hanlon as a friend. "We discovered the person responsible for both your father's and Joe Dennis's deaths."

"Who?" they all asked simultaneously.

"Judge Hanlon."

The room got completely quiet and then it was Shondra who spoke. "There must be some mistake, Drey. The judge is like a godfather to all of us. He and Dad were good friends. He would never hurt Dad."

"He did, Shondra, and a warrant is already in the works for his arrest."

Tyson was out of his seat in a flash. "Damn, I hope you're wrong because what we didn't say earlier is that Hanlon is here, with Mom in the flower garden. He's joining us for dinner."

Everyone turned toward the French doors, ready to run, when a smiling Evelyn appeared with the judge by her side. Her smile widened when she saw Drey. "Drey, how are you? Glad you could visit. You know Judge Hanlon, don't you?"

The room got silent. Drey narrowed his gaze. "Yes, I know him."

Drey followed the judge's eyes. He was staring at Charlene, probably remembering her from the store at the mall earlier and was probably wondering why she was there. Drey decided to make introductions. "And this is a friend of mine, Charlene Anderson."

Forever the gracious hostess, Evelyn smiled and said, "Welcome to our home, Charlene."

"Thank you."

With all the niceties out of the way, Drey turned his attention back to the judge. "This is a coincidence, Judge Hanlon. You're just the person I want to see. I believe you have something that belongs to the coroner's office."

The man's smile didn't quite reach his eyes when he said, "You must be mistaken."

Drey's smile was likewise. "I don't think so. Charlene works for the coroner's office and it just so happens that a key she saw on your key ring today is one that turned up missing from the coroner's office."

The judge chuckled. "That's not possible."

"It is," Drey said, getting tired of this cat-and-mouse game the judge was playing. "It's the same key that was taken out of Joe Dennis's stomach during an autopsy."

Judge Hanlon looked around to find all eyes on him. "Come on, Drey, do you expect Evelyn and the others to believe that? They've known me for years. Why would a key taken out of someone's stomach interest me?" He turned to Evelyn. "He has insulted me. Either he leaves or I will."

Evelyn looked confused. She glanced from the judge to Drey, then over to Charlene. "Drey, I don't understand, what's going on? How can you accuse the judge of something like that?"

Drey took a deep breath and then said, "Easily, Evelyn, because that's not the least of his deeds. He is also responsible for Harmon's death."

Evelyn let out a startled gasp and clutched her stomach. Then an angry look appeared on her face. "Drey, that is absurd. How dare you accuse Bruce of something like that? I'm going to have to ask you to leave right now."

"No, let him stay," Malcolm said, taking a step forward and keeping his eyes on the judge the entire time.

"Ty, Shondra and I hired Drey to uncover the truth about Dad's death," Malcolm told his mother. Then he turned to the judge. "I don't like the fact that he's accused you any more than you do. But I think we need to hear him out."

Judge Hanlon stiffened and anger exploded in his face. "What! You would take the word of your father's bastard over me?"

Startled gasps went through the room, and seeing that everyone was now staring at Drey, a smirk appeared on the judge's face. "Yes, that's right, Drey. You thought I didn't know, didn't you? Well, I found out the truth. When were you going to tell these good people that you are

Harmon Braddock's bastard child and that your mother is Daiyu Longwei, a woman he had an affair with thirty-three years ago?"

Evelyn held her hand over her heart as she continued to look at Drey. She then asked in a low and shocked voice, "It is true, Drey? Are you Daiyu's son? Was Harmon your biological father?"

Drey looked around the room at all the shocked faces. He then glanced back at Evelyn, seeing the hurt in her eyes. "Yes, Daiyu Longwei is my mother and Harmon Braddock was my biological father."

Charlene's heart went out to Drey at the same time red-hot anger exploded inside her. She knew this was not the way he had wanted his siblings to find out about him, and now this murderer, of all people, was trying to make him look like the bad guy.

Charlene crossed the room and said to the judge, "You ass!" She was angry beyond reason. "It all makes sense now."

The judge looked at her as if she were demented. "I have no idea what you're talking about."

"Well, let me enlighten you. I just figured out

the reason Congressman Braddock was trying so hard to reach Drey's mother before he was killed. It was to warn her about you. You were going to blackmail him, weren't you? You were going to expose the truth about Drey if the congressman didn't cooperate. You knew the congressman was going to turn you in and you wanted to blackmail him, the same way you blackmailed my boss into cooperating with you by falsifying documents. Joe Dennis did not die of a heart attack. He was murdered. I saw the original autopsy report myself."

"Lady, you are crazy."

"And, Judge, you are a murderer, two times over. If you're so innocent, then let us see your key ring."

"Yes, Judge, why don't you let us see your key ring?" Connor Stewart said. He moved closer to Shondra's side.

"Fine!" the judge said, fumbling into his pocket. "I'll show everyone my key ring just to prove you're crazy."

He pulled out his key ring and held it up. Charlene recognized the key immediately and pointed to it. "That's it! It's *that* one."

The judge rolled his eyes. "That's the key to my locker at the gym."

Something about the key caught Evelyn's attention. "May I see it for a minute, Bruce?"

He blinked at her request, and trying to keep his cool, he said, "Certainly, Evelyn. But like I said it's the key to my locker at the gym." He removed the key from the ring and handed it to her.

She gazed down at it. Turned it over in her hand. Studied the numbers engraved on the back. When she lifted her head and gazed at Judge Hanlon, she wore a shocked look on her face. "Where did you get this key from, Bruce?"

He shrugged. "Like I said, it's my locker key that—"

"No," she interrupted him. "It's not a locker key. It's a key that's been in the Braddock family for years and it goes to a safe hidden on the mansion grounds where Harmon kept his important papers. What are you doing with this key?"

Before anyone could blink, in a calculated move, Hanlon reached out and grabbed Charlene and held her in front of him as a shield. "Stay back or I'll kill her!"

It was then that everyone noticed the small revolver he had pulled from his jacket. He was holding it close to Charlene's head. "You think you're so smart," he said, his angry words directed at Drey. "I knew Harmon would want to protect you at all costs. The last thing he wanted was for you to know that he was your father. It would have been real simple for him to be a part of everything. But no, he wanted to play Mr. Good Guy and threaten to turn me in unless I got out of it. Hell, I didn't want to get out of it. The money was good. I liked the power. The corruption suited me just fine."

"Bruce, surely you didn't—"

"Shut up, Evelyn," Hanlon said angrily. "Yes, I had him killed. He was going to the Feds with evidence. I tried blackmailing him and it didn't work. He was going to get to Daiyu before I did. So I had to have him eliminated. Joe Dennis helped. And then he got greedy so I had to eliminate him as well."

"You killed our father?" Shondra asked, coming out of her shock. "How could you?"

He sneered. "The same way I plan to kill all of you, without batting an eye, starting with this crazy one first," he said of Charlene. "She messed things up by snooping around. There's going to be a fire and all of you will perish. The Braddock mansion will burn to the ground and no one will ask any questions because I have several firemen on the take too. Their report will reflect whatever I want it to say."

"You're the one crazy if you think we're going to stand here and let you kill us too," Malcolm said.

Hanlon smiled. "You won't have a choice. I've already called for backup. A few of Houston's finest who happen to be on my payroll," he bragged.

Sirens could be heard in the distance. "I think I hear them coming now," Hanlon said, grinning from ear to ear.

Knowing the cops that were arriving were the good cops Lavender had dispatched and not the bad ones the judge was referring to, Drey figured that he had to get Charlene out of Hanlon's clutches. He gave Malcolm a nod and as if his brother understood what he wanted him to do, Malcolm kept the man talking. Confident the ball was in his court, the judge bragged about all his illegal activities and how Harmon wanted to ruin things for him.

Too late, Hanlon noticed how close Drey had gotten him, and when he made a move to aim the gun straight at Drey, Charlene elbowed him in the side. It was just the opportunity Drey needed, and within seconds, with one jab to the judge's midsection and several quick karate kicks, the man fell flat on his face. The men in the room rushed forward and used a cord from a nearby curtain to quickly tie his hands and feet.

Lavender stormed in with several police officers on his heels, as well as a couple of FBI agents. Drey stood back to let them do their job while he pulled Charlene into his arms, wanting just to hold her and make sure she was all right. He had never felt such fear as he had when Hanlon had placed the gun to her head.

He felt several pats to his back and glanced over his shoulder to see a smiling Malcolm and Tyson. "You're going to have to teach us some of those quick moves, brother," Malcolm said, grinning.

Brother. Drey inhaled sharply and then returned their smiles. In their own way they were letting him know he was accepted as one of them. "Yes, I will have to do that."

Although later than they had planned, the Braddocks finally settled down to dinner. Drey and Charlene had been asked to stay and join them. After the last platter had been placed on the table and before it was time to say grace, Evelyn stood at the head of the table with a smile on her face to speak to everyone.

"I think all of us can say that today has been full of surprises. More than anything I am glad that the man responsible for taking Harmon from us will be dealt with. There is no doubt in my mind that justice will be served."

She then centered her gaze on Drey. "And I want to welcome a new addition to our family. At this point in my life, I don't want to let secrets from the past be allowed to shadow the present. Drey, Harmon was your father and as such, you are a Braddock. I want you to know you are welcome here any time you want. You are one of us."

Cheers went up around the table and Charlene had to fight back the tears that threaten to fall. Only a gracious woman such as Evelyn could accept what had happened thirty-three years ago, not hold it against Drey and move on. And she knew in her heart that although Drey had tried convincing her otherwise, he had wanted to belong.

Shondra stood up and said, "And while the family is all gathered together, I have a surprise of my own." She smiled brightly and then reached her hand out to Connor. He took it, kissed it and then stood beside her.

"I want all of you to be the first to know that Connor and I eloped last weekend to Vegas and got married."

Everyone was out of their seats to rush over to the happy couple and give them words of congratulations and best wishes.

When it seemed as though everyone had finally settled down, it was Tyson who got up next. He looked over at his wife, Felicia, before saying to everyone, "And Felicia and I have some wonderful news to share. We found out today that we're having a son and we plan to name him Harmon Braddock."

Charlene saw the tears glistening in Evelyn's eyes. She was getting more and more good news about her family.

Malcolm stood and chuckled. "Gloria and I don't have anything to add since all of you know about our Christmas wedding. But as we head into the final week of the campaign, we're counting on all of you, our family, to help get me into office."

More claps and cheers erupted around the table and then a few minutes later everyone finally settled down for dinner. And by the time it was over, Charlene couldn't help but think it had been one glorious affair.

It was almost eleven o'clock that night when Drey and Charlene entered his home. As soon as the door closed behind them, Drey pulled Charlene close to him and reached out and took her face in his hands. "Do you have any idea how I felt when I saw Hanlon put that gun to your head?" he asked softly.

"No, tell me," she whispered softly. She had stared into his eyes the entire time the incident had been going on and had seen the stark fear evident there. But what had touched her most was something else she could have sworn she'd seen. But she refused to jump to conclusions. She wanted him to tell her if her assumptions were correct.

"I felt like I was about to lose you," he said, breaking into her thoughts. "I was going to lose you without telling you how I feel."

She swallowed deeply. "And how do you feel, Drey?"

For a moment he didn't say anything, he just stood there and tenderly stroked her cheek while gazing into her eyes. Then he spoke. "I love you, Charlene. I didn't realize how much until today. I've been fighting it and denying it. But I can't do so any longer. I know we moved quickly in our relationship, and I'm willing to slow down for us to have a long engagement if that's what you want. But I want to marry you, Charlene. I want you to be a part of my life forever. I want to sleep every night with my body connected to yours. And more importantly, I want for you to one day love me as much as I love you."

Charlene smiled through her tears. "That day is now because I do love you, Drey. I've loved you for some time, but I was afraid to let you know it. You told me in the beginning you didn't want a wife, you wanted a bed partner."

He chuckled. "Now I want both. Will you marry me, Charlene?"

"Yes, I'll marry you," she said past the constriction in her throat.

And then Drey pulled her into his arms and

kissed her again. She was simply ecstatic. This man would be her husband, the father of her babies and her best friend. He had made her the object of his protection and now she would make him the object of her love. Totally. Completely. Forever.

Epilogue

6 months later

Charlene tried not to look any place but straight ahead while her feet moved toward the altar at her father's side. Drey, handsome as ever in his black tux, was standing there waiting for her.

The past six months had been a flurry of events. Malcolm had won his congressional seat, Tyson and Felicia had their baby and Charlene had returned to work. Because she had testified in his behalf, Nate had been given a lighter sentence after his defense attorney had proven that Judge Hanlon had blackmailed him into falsifying documents by threatening to expose an extramarital affair he'd had a few years ago. Charlene had met Daiyu and cherished their growing friendship. And then there were the Braddocks, who had welcomed her and Drey into their clan with open arms.

Charlene had wanted to keep the wedding ceremony small, but Nina would not hear of it. She wanted to go all out for her daughter and she had. Over five hundred guests attended the lavish wedding, but the only person who captured Charlene's attention was Drey.

As soon as she reached where he stood, he took her hand and gently squeezed it, his way of letting her know everything would be all right. Less than a half hour later he was proven right when the minister pronounced them man and wife and gave Drey permission to kiss his bride.

Drey turned her in his arms and not waiting for one of her bridesmaids to do the honor, he brushed her veil aside and eagerly went for her lips. The moment their mouths touched, she felt, as always, a deep connection to him. Today was the first day of their lives together and she looked forward to the many years to come.

When he released her mouth, the smile he gave her brightened her entire world, and when the minister presented them to everyone as Mr. and Mrs. Drey St. John, she knew that would be a name she would wear proudly.

She suddenly felt herself swept off her feet into big, strong, muscular arms. Where they were going on their honeymoon was a secret Drey was keeping from her. All he had said was to pack light…or not pack anything at all since he enjoyed seeing her naked.

When they reached the limo that awaited them at the front of the church he managed to get them inside beneath a shower of rice and pulled her into his lap. Then he was kissing her again and she knew there was no other place she'd rather be than in his arms.

She faced the challenge of her career…

Seducing
the matchmaker

elaine overton

Acquiring world-renowned architect Derrick Brandt as
a client is a real coup for Noelle Brown's matchmaking
service. Finding him a mate will be no picnic, but as
attraction sizzles between them, they wonder if *their*
relationship could be the perfect match.

"Elaine Overton does a wonderful job conveying her
characters' feelings, their emotional baggage and their
struggles."
—*Romantic Times BOOKreviews*
on *His Holiday Bride*

*Available the first week of November
wherever books are sold.*

KIMANI™
ROMANCE

www.kimanipress.com

KPEO0891108

She was a knockout!

LoveTKO
pamela yaye

Boxer Rashawn Bishop woos stunning
Yasmin Ohaji with finesse and fancy footwork,
and finally TKO's her resistance. But love means
making choices, and with his career on the line,
will he follow the lure of boxing…or the woman
he can't live without?

"A fun and lighthearted story."
—*Romantic Times BOOKreviews*
on Pamela Yaye's *Other People's Business*

*Available the first week of November
wherever books are sold.*

KIMANI™
ROMANCE

KPPY0911108

Breaking up is hard to do…
even when you know it's right.

NATIONAL BESTSELLING AUTHOR

marcia
King-
Gamble

first crush

Hudson Godfrey's new wine-making business leaves
him with no time for a relationship, so he breaks up with
one-of-a-kind woman Laila Stewart. Of course, he didn't
realize she would wind up moving to Washington state
and working with him. Or that their heated daytime
glances would lead to sizzling passionate nights. Now
he's starting to wonder if letting this alluring woman go
was the biggest mistake of his life….

Coming the first week of November 2008,
wherever books are sold.

ARABESQUE®

www.kimanipress.com   KPMKG1131108

"A delightful book romance lovers will enjoy."
—*Romantic Times BOOKreviews*
on *Love Me or Leave Me*

ESSENCE BESTSELLING AUTHOR

GWYNNE FORSTER

Secret desire

Their lives spared but nerves shattered in a
harrowing robbery, independent widow
Kate Middleton and her young son are rescued
by Luke Hickson, a handsome police captain still
reeling from a calamity of his own. Neither Kate nor
Luke expects, much less welcomes, their instant
attraction. But when trouble strikes again, Kate
realizes there's only one place she feels safe—
in Luke's strong embrace.

*Coming the first wefi of November 2008,
wherever books are sold.*

ARABESQUE®

www.kimanipress.com

KPGF1141108

For All We Know

NATIONAL BESTSELLING AUTHOR

SANDRA KITT

Michaela Landry's quiet summer of
house-sitting takes a dramatic turn when
she finds a runaway teen and brings him
to the nearest hospital. There she meets
Cooper Smith Townsend, a local pastor
whose calm demeanor and dedication are
as attractive as his rugged good looks.
Now their biggest challenge will be to trust
that a passion neither planned for is strong
enough to overcome any obstacle.

Coming the first week of September 2008,
wherever books are sold.

ARABESQUE®

www.kimanipress.com KPSKI040908

USA TODAY Bestselling Author

BRENDA JACKSON

invites you to discover the always sexy and always satisfying Madaris Men.

Experience where it all started…

Tonight and Forever
December 2007

Whispered Promises
January 2008

Eternally Yours
February 2008

One Special Moment
March 2008

ARABESQUE®

www.kimanipress.com

KPBJREISSUES08